N S Brooks, a qualified Chartered Accountant, spent over 40 years in London working as an accountant in practice. He started his writing career on retirement. This is his first novel. He lives in West London with his wife.

To my wife, Caroline, and all my family and friends.
I hope you will enjoy this book.

N S Brooks

BETRAYED

AUSTIN MACAULEY PUBLISHERS™
LONDON • CAMBRIDGE • NEW YORK • SHARJAH

A CIP catalogue record for this title is available from the British Library.

ISBN 9781528914659 (Paperback)
ISBN 9781528914666 (Hardback)
ISBN 9781528914673 (Kindle e-book)
ISBN 9781528960977 (ePub e-book)

www.austinmacauley.com

First Published (2019)
Austin Macauley Publishers Ltd
25 Canada Square
Canary Wharf
London
E14 5LQ

Chapter One

Will Slater stirred and stretched under the Egyptian cotton sheet. He lay in that delicious semi-sleep with some senses awake, others still comatose. His body still felt heavy on the mattress from deep sleep. Little did he know that the next 48 hours would change the rest of his life!

Will knew it would be another hot day in London, the temperature was already building up in the bedroom. It had been like this for the last 6 weeks and even though it was the end of August, there seemed to be no end to the heat wave.

In his half-sleep, he heard an early rising neighbour repairing his garden fence and in that instant, he was transported back to his childhood, lying in bed in his parents' home listening to a similar noise.

Will lay there and pondered on why sounds and smells can be so evocative of the past when sometimes he had difficulty in remembering what he had done last week!

Wonderful, the start of a weekend and nothing much to do but laze around and enjoy the sun!

A shaft of light cut through the room from the gap in the curtain, picking out a band of dust particles dancing like dervishes this way and that.

He stretched again across the double bed. He tried to remember what it had been like to share the bed with Claire, his ex-wife. It was only a couple of years, but it seemed a lifetime away now. He was not sure he really missed her. Perhaps he was still scarred by the way she had left. She had married his best friend, Toby. Apparently, they had been having an affair for years.

When Claire first told him, he just accepted it. He felt betrayed, but he never really got angry. They were two people he had loved most in his life and whatever people say, you can't just stop loving someone overnight. It was perhaps this indifference to the situation that annoyed Claire the most.

She said it was typical and just proved why she had to move on. She had gone on to say that his only interest was his work and that she and the children had always taken second place and he was always too tired for the physical side of the relationship so it was time she felt like a woman again.

It was true, sex had never been hugely important to Will and he did work long hours but it had provided all the creature comforts that the family had enjoyed. There was no question that he enjoyed the challenges of his work and he did like the substantial financial rewards that he achieved from deals that he arranged for his clients.

Claire would certainly not want materially from her new husband. Toby McCloud was a multi-millionaire property developer and as the "glossies" would say, with homes in Scotland, New York and Bermuda.

Toby and Will had been to state school together in West London. Neither came from wealthy backgrounds. Toby's father was an engineer in a brewery and Will's father was in local government. Latterly, Toby pretended that his lineage was from Scotland, which, presumably, it had been at some time, but his parents had never ventured North of Watford and Toby's first trip to Scotland was to buy his home. He spotted the house in a property magazine and purchased it without even visiting it. When he was in Scotland, he put on a Scottish accent as if he had been born and bred there. Will thought that strange because in all other ways Toby was very open and straightforward. It was as if he was denying his upbringing and pretending to be someone he wasn't. However, Toby, like Will, was intelligent and both were good sportsmen. Toby decided not to go to Uni and went straight into the building trade, eventually setting up his own development company. He didn't compete with the "big boys", he mainly just built small blocks of flats. Typically, he would purchase a large family home, demolish it and build expensive flats. Will was not sure he liked this policy but the demand for large family homes seemed to have diminished over the years.

Will, on the other hand, went to Uni, studied Law but concentrated on playing cricket whilst he was there. He was reasonably good and two counties had offered him contracts but he decided that Law was where the money was, so when he got his degree, he joined a small practice in Central London. When he was fully qualified, he joined one of the very large firms as a newly qualified solicitor. He stayed there until he left to set up his own practice.

Will continued to lie in bed and then he thought about his children. He didn't see a lot of them either. Perhaps Claire had been right, they didn't really know him. Matthew was in his last year at school and spent his holidays either with friends or in Toby's homes in New York and Scotland. Louise was in York reading modern languages and spent most of her time with her boyfriend in North London. His main contact with them was when they needed money.

Oh well, he thought, nothing much he could do about the past but made a mental note to call both the kids in the next day or so to see how they were.

Saturday! What would he do today? The grass was brown from the heat so mowing the lawn was one job that was not required. Watch the cricket on the television and then down to the local tennis club for a few sets when the temperature had dropped a little. Yes, it promised to be a relaxing day!

Will got up and looked in the full-length mirror. *Not bad for 48*, he thought, patting his stomach, *could be slimmer* but no one ever saw him naked anymore so who cared. Still, a full head of brown hair and no grey. *Overall, not in too bad a shape*, he thought.

He put on a silk dressing gown and sauntered down to the kitchen and started to make a fresh pot of percolated coffee.

The phone rang.

'Hello,' Will said into the handset.

'Will, it's Michael Bore, good morning.'

'Michael, good morning.'

Michael was one of Will's oldest and best clients. Will's practice earned hundreds of thousands of pounds every year from Michael's business dealings.

'Sorry to trouble you so early on a Saturday morning but I need to meet with you as I have had an offer for the purchase of one of my companies, the buyers are from the US and they need to tie up a few details before they fly back to the States tonight. Can we meet this morning? Shouldn't take too long.'

It was going to ruin Will's Saturday but perhaps he would still have time for his tennis later in the afternoon.

'OK Michael, let's say 10 a.m. in the office and this is going to cost you.'

'What's new, Will, I keep your practice in business with the exorbitant fees you charge me anyway. See you at ten.'

Chapter Two

Will put the top down on his convertible Mercedes SL and drove the few miles from his Wimbledon home to his office which was situated in the West End of London, just north of Oxford Street. He parked in the nearby underground car park where he had a yearly reserved place, as did all his three partners and some of his senior staff. It was expensive but it allowed everyone to be flexible in their working hours and to travel home safely when leaving the office late in the evening, which in their line of business was not unusual. Slater & Craig was a firm of lawyers who specialised in corporate finance, in fact that was all they did. Advising on the buying and selling of companies for clients. There had never been a "Craig" in the firm but when Will had set up the practice, he felt it gave a feeling of greater size and stability to add another name to the title.

The firm's clients were either publically quoted companies or entrepreneurs buying or selling businesses. The firm didn't need to advertise, their work came from either satisfied clients, who had had the benefit of the partners' hugely effective and aggressive bargaining skills, upping sale prices or decreasing purchase prices, or from those who had suffered by the same hand and didn't want to suffer again.

Will didn't have time to put the coffee on when the front door bell rang.

'Hello,' Will called through the intercom.

'Your best client here.'

'Come up, Michael.'

Michael arrived with a bundle of papers in his hand.

'Good to see you, Will, sorry it is a Saturday but the Americans are pressing and you know how they don't respect weekends.'

'That's OK, Michael, I will just double my bill for weekend work.'

'I would expect nothing less,' Michael said with a grin on his face.

'Coffee?'

'Yes, please.'

'OK, go into my office and I will bring it in.'

When Will brought the coffee back to his office, Michael was standing behind Will's desk looking out of the window. Will sensed a movement as he entered the room as if Michael had moved to the window quickly.

'Not a great view from here, Will. Now, if you came and worked for me you would have a penthouse view from your office over the Thames.'

Michael had asked Will to work for him many times, encouraging him with a large salary, profit share and less pressure. But somehow being an employee of Michael's, did not appeal to Will. He could see he might be pressurised into cutting corners and even being asked to compromise his legal ethics. Although the negotiations that he and his partners embarked on for their clients were highly commercial, they were always done correctly under law.

'No thanks, Michael, I don't want to end up in prison.'

'Sometimes, Will, everything is not what it seems and you should take advice from your friends.'

'What do you mean by that?'

'Nothing, really, but just take care.'

Will found this a strange conversation but dismissed it from his mind as irrelevant and put it down to the fact that Michael was annoyed at being turned down again. Not something that happened to him often!

'OK, job in hand, what needs to be done so urgently?' asked Will.

'Well, I have been approached by this American outfit who want to buy my plastic extrusion factory in Blackburn. You remember the one I purchased two years ago. The agreement looks OK to me but you need to go through it in detail next week. But they are having a meeting of their main board on Monday and want an agreement, in principle from me to go ahead, subject to contract, of course. However, there are certain

12

conditions that I am concerned about, particularly in connection with a number of the financial warranties that they wish me to agree to, some going back to the time before I owned the factory. If I can't sign up for them, I want to tell them today as I don't want to waste my time or yours if the deal is a non-starter.'

'OK, let's have a look at them,' said Will.

Will and Michael Bore spent the next 3 hours going through the relevant clauses of the document, cross-referring to the purchase agreement two years ago.

'OK, that about covers it, I think. Are you happy, Michael?'

'Yep, I think so. I know where I stand and what I need to get changed. I am going to shoot back to my office now and call the Americans before they leave for the airport. Thanks for your time and I will call you on Monday to let you know how things went and what the next stage is. Enjoy the rest of your weekend and sorry for impinging into it.'

With that Michael shook Will's hand and left the office.

Chapter Three

After Michael had left, Will wandered around the empty office. He had always liked being in the office by himself, which was rare these days. This was his business, he had started it and built it up and, somehow, he felt a sense of achievement. He walked around the large open-plan floor where the staff sat, with the four partners offices at each corner.

The newest Partner was Sam Brewer, he was married to a minor member of the aristocracy. An impoverished aristocratic family by all accounts and Sam's drive was to keep his overbearing wife, Philiida, and four young children in the style that they had never had but believed was part of their right. Still, it meant that Sam worked every hour he could to pay for his huge rambling house in Sussex, the school fees, the Caribbean holidays, the horses, the nanny and the gardener. He earned well but Will did wonder sometimes how Sam made ends meet.

Sam Brewer was educated at Eton School and Oxford University and had a slightly academic air about him with longish flowing hair, a dishevelled appearance and a distinct stoop to his thin 6'6" frame. His office followed the same dishevelled pattern with a sophisticated floor filing system with piles of paperwork representing the deals he was working on, some of the paperwork flowing onto the neighbouring pile. Will suspected some of the piles represented deals that were also long finished. Sam always ensured Will that any confidential papers were locked away each night. Even if they weren't, it would take a clever person to work their way around the mountains of paperwork.

Whatever the outward appearance showed, there was no wooliness in Sam's brain with a 1st in Economics from Exeter College and fluent in two foreign languages, which he had taught himself in his spare time whilst travelling to the countries for holidays when a student.

Sam was particularly effective around the negotiating table, for those who didn't know him, he appeared often naïve, gathering information for his clients from the other party that should have most probably remained undisclosed, only to have it later returned to them with rapier precision either upping or cutting the price depending on whether his client was selling or buying.

Will closed the door on the chaos and strolled across to the office that was directly opposite from his and was inhabited by another of Will's Partners, Sara Crombie. Will always had a soft spot for Sara, perhaps even a romantic fancy in his dreams! He admired her intelligence and her determination to succeed. She was not afraid to use her feminine charm to win over the opposition. It never amazed him how gullible businessmen could be. Just because the other side's lawyer was a very attractive woman who oozed sex appeal, didn't mean that she wouldn't "screw" the last penny out of a deal for her client. That is what Sara did best!

Sara's office was a complete antithesis to Sam's, not a paper in sight anywhere. Will traced an imaginary line with his finger over the smooth mahogany of Sara's desk, which in one corner had a photograph frame of her husband, Peter, wearing military attire leaning against a jeep in some distant part of the world. Will had never liked Peter, he could never see what Sara had seen in him. He always seemed to be angry about something, whether it was the job he used to do in the Services or because he had a much darker side, Will was never sure. He now seemed to travel all over the world advising governments on security.

By all accounts, their children had taken after Peter, not only in their red-headed appearance but in their aggressiveness to their fellow man. Justin, their eldest, has twice been excluded from school for beating up another pupil and Chloe was sent to boarding school to see if the nuns could knock some decorum into her.

The next office, making up the square, belonged to George Wright, the first partner that Will had appointed. George was a bull of a man, although he was shorter than Sam at six foot four, he was very heavily built with a 19-inch neck and weighing in at around 17 stone. Immaculately dressed in his hand made shirts and suits from Jermyn Street, he often looked wealthier than some of the entrepreneurial clients that he represented. But the one similar feature of all Will's partners was that they were never quite what they seemed and you underestimated them at your own cost. Something that, perhaps, Will should have taken note of himself.

George was no exception to the rule. George had an air of someone who had stepped out of the pages of Debrett's but in fact had come from a tough South London working class family. It was reputed that his father had spent time in prison. Will had met George soon after qualifying when both were working at one of the "Magic Circle" firms of solicitors. They worked on a number of deals together making a lot of money for the partners but with no financial benefit for themselves. So they both thought, why do this for others? Will had more resources than George, so he agreed to leave first, set up a firm, obtain some initial clients and then George would join.

George's negotiating style would generally consist of launching into the opposing side at the table calling them numpties and threatening to advise his clients to seek a deal elsewhere with people whom at least could understand the simplest elements of business finance. Even his own clients occasionally feared him, not for their own personal safety but that they might witness or be party to a grievous wounding of the other side's lawyers or clients. Just sitting in a chair, he looked enormous but when he stood up, which he did frequently if he was not getting his own way in the negotiations; he would place himself strategically in front of the window and the light seemed to dim as if an ominous omen was about to cast its evil spell over the assembled audience. Some of his clients referred to him as "pit-bull", probably not to his face, but once you had been on the opposite side of the negotiating table, you only ever returned to his side. Will didn't always like George's clients, he thought they often appeared shifty and on more than one occasion, he got the impression that they might have criminal tendencies. George always denied this and the fees billed were large and always got paid.

Despite George's manner, he was inwardly a shy man and kept his personal life to himself but was reputed to have many female friends.

Of course, George's type of negotiating only worked for certain clients and certain deals. Will's approach was entirely different and was based on common sense rather than intimidation and appealed to clients who were somewhat less aggressive in their business dealings and were seeking more harmonious relations with their future business partners. But Will was tough and his clients never completed a deal feeling that they had not maximised their position.

Will was just about to leave George's office when he noticed a file had been caught in one of George's desk drawers, as if he had hurriedly tried to put it away and close the drawer. Will opened the drawer to put it straight when he noticed the name on the file "Java PLC". The file was empty, which seemed strange. He made a mental note to ask George on Monday, not knowing that by Monday this would be the last thing on his mind. Will put the file flat in the drawer and closed it.

Will felt hungry, so rather than go straight home, he left the office and walked around the corner to a small Italian restaurant. As luck would have it, there was a table outside on the pavement. Will ordered a Mediterranean salad and a San Miguel to accompany the "Mediterranean" weather. He spent the next hour watching people saunter by in the sun.

Will drove home slowly. There was something about a late, hot summer Saturday afternoon in London. He was not quite sure what it was. Everything seemed to move much slower. Whether it was the heat or that the pavements were mostly occupied by tourists. But there was a sort of tranquil peace not normally associated with London.

As Will opened his front door, the phone was ringing, he was not expecting a call and had a premonition that it would not be good news somehow. *Oh well*, he thought, *the day's ruined now, it can't get any worse, whoever wants me!*

Chapter Four

'Will? It's Toby,' the voice said at the other end of the phone.

'Hello, Toby.'

It had been many months since Will had spoken to his ex-wife's new husband and his ex-best friend!

Will could tell that Toby had been in Scotland for a while as he was using his Scottish accent.

'Ach, I need to see yee and give yee something very urgently. I think we are all in big trouble. Can yee fly up tomorrow?'

'What's happened? Is it the children or Claire?'

'No, nothing to do with them but it will affect us all. I canne tell yee over the phone. I think they are listening.'

'Toby, what is this all about? You can't expect me to drop everything and fly up to the Highlands of Scotland without some more information!'

'I know I have done wrong by yee with Claire but I am desperate and if you don't come, anything might happen. Please, Will. I would'ne ask if it was not a matter of life and death and if not mine then maybe yours.'

'Come on, Toby, don't be so melodramatic.'

'Fly to Glasgow and pick up a hire car. I will expect to see you about mid-day tomorrow.'

And with that the line went dead.

Will stood by the phone with the receiver to his ear and listened to the dialling tone.

He redialled Toby but just got the engaged signal!

This was mad. It wasn't in his nature to just charge off somewhere without a good reason or having planned it in advance. But somehow he felt compelled to go and deep down inside there was an uneasy feeling beginning to climb into his subconscious.

Chapter Five

Will got an early morning British Airways flight to Glasgow and tracked down a car hire booth, which he hoped would have a car for him there and then.

'Good morning. Have you got a car available that I can have immediately, please?' asked Will.

'Ach, that we have sir. What sort of car would you be wanting?'

'I hadn't thought of anything, perhaps automatic and something with a bit of oomph, as I have got a long drive to Ballachulish in the Highlands.'

'Ay, yee have a long drive, sir. But it is a beautiful day. May I suggest a Class E vehicle, an Audi or a Merc?'

'Have you got a soft top as the weather is so good?'

'The only one I have is an Audi A3.'

'That's fine, thank you.'

Will paid on his credit card and followed the directions to the pick-up point.

Will had done this journey to see Toby on a few occasions before and he remembered the most difficult part was getting from the Airport to Dumbarton after that it was a pretty easy. He threaded his way through the airport roads, over the Erskine Bridge and on to the A82. He stopped at Arden on the southernmost part of Loch Lomond, put the roof down and then enjoyed the magnificent views up the side of the Loch. He remembered the first time he had travelled this road, many years ago and was breath-taken by the different views that were exposed each time the road twisted and turned along the loch side. The road had improved since then and some of the surprise was no longer there but the view remained the same. The rich blue of the deep loch, with the sun picking up the crests of small waves like little starbursts. The white sands of little beaches on the far side leading to vivid green uplands and then the mountains in various shades of brown standing like sentries guarding a royal view. The road swept north, up the side of the Loch passing exotic sounding places, Tarbet, Inverglas, Ardlui and Inverarnan and at Crianlarich he turned left and headed towards Rannoch Moor, Glencoe and his final destination Ballachulish.

Will stopped at the Bridge of Orchy Hotel for a break. He got out of the car and gazed through the clear bright light at the road ahead as it snaked through the Moor and up into the canyon that was Glencoe. Even in bright sunlight Rannoch Moor was one of the most inhospitable places he had ever seen. A terrain of lochs, lochans, peat bogs and streams as far as he could see, with rugged and jagged rocks peeking out from purple, brown and green pools of heather and gorse. A truly wild place but the bleakness had its own beauty and Will pondered that the view he saw on either side of the road would have been unchanged for probably thousands of years.

In the doorway to the hotel, there were tourist leaflets and Will picked up one for the Rannoch Moor and Glencoe area. From the leaflet, Will read that the novelist Robert Louis Stevenson referred to Rannoch Moor in his novel *Kidnapped* as "A wearier looking desert a man never saw".

Will went into the bar and ordered a coffee.

There was only one other person in the bar, an elderly man who had an empty glass in front of him and appeared to be asleep. He reminded Will of the mole character from the book *Wind in the Willows*. As the barman placed a cup of coffee in front of Will, he heard a voice that seemed to be addressed to him.

'Yee up from down South,' said the voice from the mole who had silently and somewhat disconcertingly moved his position at the bar to sit next to Will.

'Yes,' said Will.

'Yee'll be up to see the Glen then?' said the voice again in a quiet Scottish brogue.

'Do you mean Glencoe?'

'Aye, I do laddie. Everyone who comes this far north visits the Glen.'

'I expect you know all the history about Glencoe?' Will ventured.

'Aye, I do that. I was a guide up at the Visitor Centre for 15 years after I retired from the sea. Evil place it be. Some days, I could hear the cries of the slaughtered in the wind,' the old man said.

'Tell me more about the massacre that occurred there?' asked Will. 'Can I buy you another drink?'

'Aye, that would be kind. A half of heavy and a large single malt please.'

Will placed the order with the barman and smiled to himself. He was sure that the old man had only been drinking a beer and not a whisky as well.

'So, tell me about the massacre,' Will said again wanting to get some value for his purchase.

'Well, it all started,' the old man said, 'on or about 1 February 1692, two companies of red-coated government soldiers, about 120 men, of whom around a dozen were Campbells were sent to Glencoe. The commander of the government forces was a Captain Robert Campbell. He was welcomed to the glen, and he and his soldiers were sheltered and fed amongst the various cottages in the area. Many people think that it was the MacDonalds that were massacred but actually it was the Maclains, who were part of the Donald clan and were related through marriage.'

The old man stopped and drank a mouthful of whisky and washed it down with a swig of bitter.

He went on, 'At 5 a.m. on the morning of 13 February, Campbell and his redcoats set about carrying out their orders. Whether due to incompetence or some of the soldiers not being enthusiastic for the task, only 38 men, women and children out of the 200 in the clan were killed, though others perished later on the snow-swept hills as they tried to escape. Some were shot in the back and the rings from the hand of the chief's wife were hacked off – she died soon after.'

'Aye,' said the old man, 'the Highlands were a rough and tough place and the Campbells had suffered their own disasters at the hands of other clans but what was unforgivable was that Campbell and his men had enjoyed the traditional Highland hospitality before turning on their hosts who included Campbell's own niece and her husband.'

'But what was the reason behind the killing in the first place?' asked Will.

'Aye, well, Glencoe had been home to the MacDonalds,' the old man went on, 'since at least the early 14th century when they supported King Robert, the Bruce of Scotland. The chief of the MacDonalds of Glencoe was Alasdair MacDonald, known as Maclain. He was reputed to have been a huge man with flowing white hair, beard and moustache. He was well respected by his own clan and feared by others – very much an old-school highland chief. The Maclains were constantly involved in trouble with the law and with neighbouring clans for their consistent raiding, pillaging and cattle rustling. The clan had particular trouble with neighbouring Campbell clans.'

The old man stopped, had a rattling cough and knocked back his whisky. Will felt this was a sign and offered to buy the old man a refill. This was again gratefully accepted. When both replenished glasses were settled down on the bar in front of him the old man continued.

'There were many Highland clans at the time in the 15th century who were a possible threat to the new regime in London under King William of Orange, and many who openly swore their allegiance to the deposed Stuart King – James VII. King William himself was more concerned with his war against the French King, Louis XIV. Problems in the Highlands were little more than a nuisance to him.'

Another pause for sustenance and the old man progressed.

'The Donald clan was a huge force within the Highland clan system, of which, the MacDonalds of Glencoe or as I said before, the Maclains, as they were more specifically known, were only a small part.

'An order came through that the chiefs were to sign an oath of allegiance to King William by January 1, 1692. Although this oath was originally packaged with the promise of money and land for the clans, by the time it was circulated publicly, the terms were much more threatening – the clans would sign the agreement or be punished with the "utmost extremity of the law". The man who used this deadline to his own political ends was the Secretary of State, John Dalrymple, Master of Stair, who was a Lowlander and a Protestant. He disliked the Highlanders and viewed their whole way of life as a hindrance to Scotland, which would be better served, he thought, in union with England. He had a particular dislike for the MacDonalds of Glencoe.

'Another problem for the clans at the time was the fact that many of them were bound by an oath to James Stuart, the deposed King in France. It was December 12 before James had released the clans from their oath and December 28 before a messenger arrived in the Highlands with the news − leaving only three days until the deadline.'

Another rattling cough and another swig from both glasses.

'As the worst of winter swept through Glencoe on December 31, Maclain, fearful for the safety of his clan, left for Fort William to sign the oath. From here he was turned back by Colonel John Hill, who explained that the oath had to be taken before a sheriff. This involved a 60-mile trek to Inveraray: the principle town of his enemies, the Campbells. Still Maclain could have met the deadline had he not been captured by Campbell soldiers serving in the Duke of Argyll's regiment. They detained him for a day and then for several more days in Inveraray due to the absence of the Sheriff, Sir Colin Campbell. Even then, Maclain had to plead with the Sheriff to accept the late oath.

'In Edinburgh, the Master of Stair, with his legal team, declined the late-delivered oath. Everything was ready for the fall, which Stair had engineered, for the clan. The orders were explicit: the MacDonalds were to be slaughtered − "cut off root and branch". Three commanders were to be involved − two from the Campbell-dominated Argyll regiment and one from Fort William. In the end, two of those never arrived in time, claiming delay through bad weather. It was Captain Robert Campbell of Glenlyon, a desperate man who lost all his wealth through gambling, who carried out Stair's final order: "to put all to the sword under seventy".'

Will was fascinated by the details that the old man had in his head and delivered in such a tone that Will could conjure up in his own mind a picture of the events as they unfolded. He offered another round while he had a second coffee.

'Please go on,' Will suggested.

'Aye, I will laddie as you seem very interested.'

'As I said earlier, the soldiers arrived at Glencoe twelve days before the massacre, as friends, seeking shelter due to the fact that the fort was full. The MacDonalds, honouring the Highland hospitality code, duly gave the soldiers quarter in their own houses. For twelve days they lived together with neither the clan nor the Argyll soldiers knowing what lay ahead.

'On the night of February 13, a blizzard howled through Glencoe, giving whiteout conditions. As the clan slept, the houseguests gathered, received their orders and set about systematically killing everyone they could. Thirty-eight lay dead the next morning, including the chief, Maclain. Many more escaped into the hills, some finding shelter before the elements could kill them, some, including Maclain's elderly wife, died on the mountainside.

'It seemed certain that some of the Campbell soldiers, disgusted with their orders, alerted the families who had been their hosts, giving them time to escape and at least wrap up against the blizzard. Many historians also claim that the lateness of the other two companies of soldiers who were to help in the slaughter was deliberate − a ploy not to be involved in such an atrocity.

'The nation of Scotland, although used to war and murder in its many forms, was outraged by the callousness of the massacre of Glencoe. For the Jacobites in Edinburgh, it was a powerful piece of anti-government propaganda. An inquiry was held and Scottish Parliament declared the whole affair an act of murder. John Dalrymple, the Master of Stair, resigned and the matter was forgotten by the government. In Scotland, it passed into legend. The Campbells were accursed in much of the Highlands and even to this day the old Clachaig Inn at Glencoe carries the sign on its door, "No Campbells".'

'I suppose today it would be called "ethnic cleansing",' retorted Will.

'Aye, laddie I believe it would.'

'Well, thank you for a very interesting history lesson. My name is Will Slater,' Will said holding out his hand.

'Pleasure to meet you laddie, thank yee for the wee drams. I would've told yee the story without. Hamish Campbell is my name.'

They shook hands and Will went back to his car.

Chapter Six

Will continued on the A82 northwards towards the slightly foreboding mouth of the massive glen. Every few yards along the sides of the road were "whiteout poles" looking like large lollypops which were supposed to show drivers the way in snowy conditions. In the brilliant sunlight, it was difficult to imagine their need. Towards the top of the climb on the road to the Glen, there was a lay-by where a number of cars and motor bikes had stopped to admire the view. Will pulled in also and got out of the car to look back at the Moor. He could see the road he had travelled stretch out like thin tape as it ran South and then West past the hotel where he had stopped and into the distance towards Crianlarich and beyond.

Will drove on. Initially, the sides of the glen were steep with towering reddish-brown cliffs. At regular intervals, there were cars tucked into the side of the road where their occupants were engaged in the scaling of the rock faces. The glen then gave way to a more gentle terrain, still rugged but where Will could imagine the Donald clan lived in their cottages on the hillsides. Will pressed on to Ballachulish, the next stop.

The town of Ballachulish is situated on both the north and south sides of Loch Leven. Until 1975, when a bridge was finally built at the western end of the Loch, a ferry used to join the two parts of the town. Those not wanting to join the queue for the ferry, had a fifteen-mile detour around the loch via Kinlochleven. It was this route that Will took as Toby McCloud's house was on the South side of the Loch looking north towards Fort William and Ben Nevis. The house was half way along the road between the turn off and Kinlochleven. Will pulled into the drive through a five bar gate which was open. The drive in fact was merely a large gravel rectangle where a good number of cars could have been parked. There were, in fact, only two cars parked in the drive. One was a brand new Range Rover, which he assumed was Toby's, the other a small nondescript model. Will parked his hire car next to them.

He rang the doorbell. There was no reply, so he decided to walk around to the back of the house via the garden, thinking that Toby was probably on the sun terrace at the rear. The house was impressive if not beautiful. The original 19th-century house, bought from a photograph, had become run down and Toby had spent a considerable amount of money in renovating it. It was a double-fronted house built in typical grey Scottish granite. The house was built in the middle of the plot with gardens on three sides and the drive in the front. A separate detached double garage had been added to the left of the house. The views from the front of the house were to the north, over Loch Leven and towards Ben Nevis. The back of the house was south facing and warmer with views across moorland towards Glencoe. In good weather, as it was today, it was difficult to picture a more beautiful place, if you liked isolation. However, in winter, Will thought it would be very lonely and could imagine the souls of the dead MacDonalds roaming the land around the house. A slight shiver worked its way through Will's body as he walked through the garden gate to the right side of the house. The garden had been walled on its western side, presumably to provide some protection from the weather, as the eastern side was protected by woods. Immediately, through the gate on the right, was a large vegetable garden consisting of what Will imagined would be early winter vegetables, runner beans on bamboo tripod frames and various type of herbs. Will could see his ex-wife's hand at work. Further on there were spectacular borders, which in the South would have been passed their best, but up here they were still in their pomp. Delphiniums, lupins, hollyhocks, salvias, lysmachia plus many other species all fighting for their patch of earth. The lawn between the borders and the path that flowed its way around the side of the house was immaculate and looked as if it had been cut that day. The garden at the southern boundary had a wire mesh fence to keep the deer out. The positioning of the fence had been cleverly designed as it was a few yards from the boundary edge of the plot, covered from sight by plants and scrubs and then beyond the fence was a low hedge, marking the actual boundary leading into the moorland. So the impression was that there was no dividing line between the garden and the moor that one just transgressed into the other. Will stopped and stared at the beauty for a minute.

At the back of the house was a large patio with a table and chairs ready for entertaining. To one side was a patio heater which Will suspected was needed more often than not in these climes. As there was no one at the rear of the house he tried the conservatory doors but these were locked. So was the kitchen door further around the terrace.

Just then Will heard a muffled sound, rather like a champagne cork being released from its bottle. But the sound has an eerie feel to it and for some reason Will felt a shiver run through his body and the need to get into the house as soon as possible. He started running towards the front of the house when he heard a car door slam and the revving of an engine and as he got to the side gate, the smaller of the two cars in the drive was speeding towards the road churning dirt and gravel in its wake.

The front door had been left half open. Will entered.

'Toby,' called Will. 'Are you there?'

'Toby, it's Will, where are you?' called Will again.

There was no answer. The house felt very still and quiet but, somehow, not peaceful.

Will started to walk through the house towards the back. Immediately, through the front door on either side of the hall were large alcoves or vestibules. The one on the left, housed Toby's gun safe and a baby grand piano. The one on the right had a couple of comfortable looking chairs and was where the stairs started to the next floor. Past each vestibule were large rooms on either side of the house. The left one was Toby's study and looked over the woods on the eastern edge of the property but there was no sign of Toby in there. The one on the right, which was the dining room, was also empty apart from a massive dining table and chairs and looked out over the flower borders.

Will called again and continued to walk down the hall towards the rear of the house. His foot kicked something on the floor; he bent down and picked up a small key which he placed on the shelf over the radiator.

'Toby, it's Will.' But there was still no reply.

The next room on the right was the lounge, which was also empty of human life as was the conservatory beyond the lounge.

The opposite side on the left was what the Scots called a "snug" and was the less formal lounge with a huge television acting as the focal point and a couple of well-worn settees angled towards the TV.

The next door was to the cellar and Will thought he would leave that to the end if there was no sign of Toby.

The next room on the left was the kitchen which he knew, from Claire, had been recently fitted out. There was a peculiar and somewhat unpleasant smell emanating from the room as he entered.

From a first look it also seemed empty but as Will walked towards the island work surface, he realised there was something on the floor on the other side. He looked and recoiled in horror, not believing his eyes. He looked again. Toby was sitting on the floor, leaning back against the washing machine. He had a neat red hole in the middle of his forehead and a slick of red liquid ran down the front of the washing machine, collecting in a puddle on the kitchen floor which was slowly surrounding the inert body of Toby.

Will backed away in horror and revulsion. He felt sick. He pulled his mobile phone out of his pocket but there was no signal so he used the phone in the hall to call the police.

Chapter Seven

Will waited outside for the police to arrive. He could not stand being in the house. He lent against the hire car. He was unsure how long the police would take to arrive. If they came from Fort William, perhaps 20 minutes, he was trying to visualise how far Fort William was. Maybe an ambulance would arrive first. He had no doubt that Toby was dead although he had not taken his pulse.

After about 10 minutes, a blue Ford Focus pulled through the gate and over the gravel stopping alongside Will's car. Two men got out.

'Mr Slater?' said the shorter of the two.

'Yes.'

'My name's Harry Allan and this is my colleague, Stuart Brown,' both flashing warrant cards.

'You got here very quickly.'

'Indeed, we did sir, we were down the road and heard your call via the controller,' replied Allan.

Allan was a short rugged man, probably in his fifties with a large nose that was lined with red veins and seemed to shine like a red beacon on his craggy face.

Brown was, on the other hand, six feet four and had a huge swathe of bright red hair, the colour of carrots.

Will noticed that despite their difference in appearance they both had one thing in common – menacing eyes – that seemed to pierce straight through Will. For the second time that afternoon Will shivered involuntary.

'So Mr Slater, you say you have discovered Mr McCloud's body?'

'Yes, he is in the kitchen, he seems to have been shot.'

'Ummm, I see,' said Allan.

'Well, are you not going to check?' William almost exclaimed.

Allan and Brown exchanged glances and Allan nodded. Brown loped off inside the house.

'The killer has gone, I heard him drive off,' stammered Will.

'Can you describe the person for me?'

'Well, no, I was at the back of the house when I heard, what I think was the shot, I ran round to the front but he had driven off.'

'So you didn't see the person at all? How do you know it was a man and not a woman?' asked Allan.

'Well, I just assumed it was a man.'

'Hmmm. Did you get the registration of the car at all?'

'No, I am afraid I didn't.'

'What was the make and colour?' pressed Allan.

'Toyota, I think, or some small Japanese car. I didn't take much notice. It was dark blue,' said Will thankful that he could remember something.

'Not a lot to be going on, sir,' said Allan.

'Well, no, but that is all there is,' replied Will.

Brown appeared and nodded to Allan.

'My colleague agrees with you, Mr McCloud is dead. So Mr Slater, how do you know Mr McCloud, or should I say knew him?'

'Do you think I could sit down as I think I am suffering from shock and feel a little faint? I would rather not go into the house, could we sit in my car?' asked Will.

Allan gestured to the passenger seat and got in behind the wheel.

Will turned towards Allan and began.

'Toby, that's Mr McCloud, was for many years, my best friend. We went to school together and I helped him build up his business, I am a lawyer, and I found and advised on acquisitions for his business. However, I discovered a couple of years ago that he was having an affair with my wife.'

'I see,' said Allan in a non-committal tone.

'Well, my wife and I divorced and Toby married my wife, ex-wife, last year.'

'So you decided to kill him, sir. I can understand that,' said Allan.

'No, no, of course not, I didn't kill him.'

'Then who did?' asked Allan.

'I don't know, surely that is your job.'

'So what was your reason for this visit, I assume you don't live locally, sir.'

'No, I live in London. Toby called last evening and begged me to come up, a matter of life or death, he said.'

'Well, he wasn't wrong, was he, sir?' replied Allan cynically.

'You don't really think I did it, do you officer?' queried Will.

'Well, you are my only suspect at the moment and you would appear to have a motive.'

'If I had killed him, why would I have phoned the police?'

'In my experience, murderers often do strange things, sir. So I would not discount that entirely.'

'Am I under arrest then?' asked Will.

'Not at this moment, sir, but I would rather you didn't leave the country and I will want you to make a formal statement. Are you going back to London?'

'Yes, but probably not until tomorrow now.'

'Okay.'

'Does that mean I can go now?' Will enquired.

'Yes, you are free to go for now,' Allan said rather ominously.

Allan got out of the hire car and Will changed seats. He started the car, turned it around and headed for the road, he looked in his rear view mirror and saw Allan and Brown staring after him. Will thought that, regrettably, it was unlikely to be the last he saw of that pair. As he drove down the road, he could hear the sound of police sirens approaching from further down the Loch. Will thought that if they are coming here, they are a bit late.

Chapter Eight

Will was in a state of shock and he knew he needed to stop and rest for the night. He had noticed a hotel in Ballachulish and decided to stay there. The hotel was on the main road and he pulled into the car park of the Ballachulish Hotel. It was the sort of hotel that Will would like to stay in during the winter. Roaring log fires and typical Scottish hospitality. However, at the moment, all he wanted was somewhere to have a drink and rest.

The hotel had been modernised inside, as its old traditional red-bricked exterior gave way to a bright spacious interior. In a way, Will was a bit disappointed as his mood would have suited how he imagined the interior would have looked twenty years ago, heavy dark red curtains, tartan carpets and flock wallpaper.

He asked at the reception desk for the biggest room they had as he hated small claustrophobic rooms.

'We have a large feature room overlooking the Loch, sir,' informed the elderly and stooped male receptionist who looked as if he had been overlooked in the upgrade.

'Thank you, I will take it.'

'How will yee be paying?'

'On a credit card,' Will added, 'I wasn't planning to stay so I don't have any bags. Do you have a toothbrush that I can buy?'

The receptionist looked at Will in an old-fashioned way. It was as if Will had asked whether the receptionist knew of any "ladies" that could entertain him that night.

'I will have one taken to your room, sir.'

'Where is the bar, please?'

'Ay, yee will be wanting the Bulas Bar,' said with almost a distaste to the name. 'Through that door there, sir,' he said pointing to a large oak panelled door to the right of the reception.

'What does "Bulas" mean?' asked Will.

'I havenae a clue, sir' came the reply, which Will thought strange considering the man worked there. Probably a change that he did not approve of and was not going pander to the new concept.

'Will yee be eating here tonight?'

'Yes, I will, thank you.'

'Dinner is 7 to 10 p.m. and breakfast 7 to 9.30a.m,' said the receptionist in his lilting almost sing song accent.

'Thank you,' repeated Will and made his way to bar.

The bar was empty as it was still early and there was no sign of anyone behind the bar either. Will waited and looked at the large array of whiskies on display. While he was deciding which malt to have, the same man appeared behind the bar.

'What will yee be having, sir? A wee malt?' obviously having seen Will's line of vision.

'I will have a Talisker please, large one. Thanks.'

'Certainly, sir. Have yee had a gude day?'

'No, actually it has been awful.'

'Ach, sorry to hear that, sir.'

Will knocked back the whisky and asked for a refill before the man had time to shuffle his way back to the reception desk.

Will took his drink into the lounge and sat at a table overlooking the Loch. Will suddenly felt terribly tired and just stared out of the window. It was difficult to comprehend what had happened. Yesterday, he hadn't too many cares. Today he was a suspected murderer. Although Will knew he hadn't killed Toby, he could see how the police might suspect him. He had a motive, although why wait until now to kill Toby? The time would have been soon after he learnt about his affair with Claire. However, more worryingly was the fact that Toby had been murdered by someone and Will was connected in some way. Why did Toby want to see him? What was Toby going to tell him? Toby had said it was a matter of life and death, which unfortunately turned out to be only too true. But what was Toby involved in to cause this reaction and why was Will involved? It made no sense at all.

Will realised that it was hours since he had eaten and decided to take an early dinner and then early to bed. At 7 p.m. Will went into the Bistro dining room and sat at another table with beautiful views across the Loch. The sun was now beginning to set and he watched the seagulls darting in and out of the water catching their supper.

While Will waited for his dinner, he read the short history of the area printed on the back of the menu.

The short text explained: *Ballachulish is best known for one of its locals, a James Stewart, who was hanged in 1752 for the killing of Colin Campbell, an event used for the basis of "Kidnapped", Robert Lewis Stevenson's novel. Apparently, Stewart's guilt for the Appin Murder, as it is known, remains in doubt some 250 years after his execution.*

Will hoped that Toby's death was not anther murder where the wrong person was convicted.

Chapter Nine

Will arrived home in Wimbledon later the following day to hear the phone ringing.

'Hello.'

'Why did you kill him?' the voice of his ex-wife, Claire, screamed down the phone.

'I didn't kill him. I found his body.'

'The police said that you were there and it was suspicious. Why were you in Scotland?'

'He asked me to go. He said it was very urgent.'

'What, on a Sunday?'

Will ignored that question.

'Have you told the children?' Will asked.

'What, tell them that their father has murdered their step-father?'

'I didn't do it, Claire. You must believe me.'

'Of course, I have told them and I didn't give them any more details other than you were there at the time and the police were investigating. What am I going to do?' sobbed Claire down the phone.

Will was not sure what else he could say. He was sure that Claire would be more than capable of working out what she had to do next and momentarily he reminded himself that she was the one that had the affair and left him. At that moment the doorbell rang.

'I have to go, Claire, there's someone at the door. I will call you back.' With a sigh of relief, Will put the phone down.

Will opened the front door.

'Mr Slater? Mr William Slater?' the large burly man at the front door asked.

'Yes,' replied Will.

'I am Inspector Dawkin and this is Sergeant Edgar, may we come in, sir, to discuss the death of Mr Toby McCloud?'

Both men waved their warrant cards to indicate their identity.

'Can I see those, please?' asked Will, indicating to the warrant cards that were being placed back into the policemen's pockets.

With some hesitation and a certain amount of reluctance both men passed their identity badges across to Will.

Will scrutinised the warrant cards, looking up at each man and comparing their faces with their pictures. He then passed them back to the two men who took them rather ungratefully.

Dawkin had an unhealthy bloated face and, in fact, he had the features of a man who probably ate poorly, drank too much beer and did little exercise. However, in that moment on the doorstep, it was like looking at a poorly taken photograph. Everything about Dawkin was clearly defined and larger than life, whereas his sidekick, Sergeant Edgar, appeared fuzzy and almost looked out of focus. *Probably, the way they were in life*, thought Will.

Will shook his head as to clear his vision.

'May we come in, please, sir?' repeated Dawkin. 'Or would you like to answer our questions down at the station?'

'Yes, come in.'

Will led the two policemen into the lounge. Will had very little dealings with policemen in his line of the law but he knew instinctively that Dawkin was the type of policeman that he most disliked, arrogant, opinionated and downright rude.

Not surprisingly, Dawkin shared the same opinion of Will and had learnt that professional people, although generally law-abiding, often treated the police with a very low level of respect when in close dealings.

Will indicated the two men to sit on the settee. Dawkin seem to spread out, leaving Edgar crammed into one corner of the settee.

'We would like to get the details of the events surrounding the death of Mr Toby McCloud,' asked Dawkin with an edge to his voice.

Will gave his version of events starting with the call from Toby pleading for him to go to Scotland to the discovery of the body.

'Would you know why anyone would want to kill Mr McCloud?' Dawkin asked.

'No, since he married my wife we have lost touch.'

'I understand, he was a close friend of yours until you discovered he was having an affair with your wife.'

'Well, yes, we had known each other for years. We were in school together.'

'You must have been very upset when you found out, about the affair,' added Dawkin.

'Yes, I was. But not enough to kill him,' replied Will.

'I didn't say you had, sir, but did you?'

'No, I did not, Inspector.'

'Can I ask why you left the scene of the crime after calling the police? You should have waited for the police to arrive. We had to trace you from your mobile phone number,' stated Dawkin.

'I didn't leave the crime scene, two policemen arrived – ummm, Allan and Brown were their names. They said I could go.'

'I am afraid there are no policemen of those names who attended the scene on that day, sir.'

'Well, that's ridiculous, they showed me their warrant cards.'

'Did you look at them as closely as you looked at ours?' asked Dawkin.

'Well, no I didn't as it happens. I think I must have been in shock and was very relieved that someone else was there.'

'Well, I am afraid that they weren't policemen, sir, and it is an offense to leave the scene of the crime without giving your details. I understand you are a solicitor, so you will know that already. However, a car, with two men in it, was seen leaving the house just as two of the local lads arrived. Unfortunately, they didn't stop them. So for the moment, Mr Slater, we will believe your version of events. Nevertheless, we would like you to accompany us to the station to make a full statement, please.'

'What, now?' asked Will.

'Yes, now sir, thank you.'

Chapter Ten

'Well, talk me through the whole event, please, Mr Slater,' asked Dawkin in an interview room at the police station.

Will explained the whole series of events from the telephone call on Saturday afternoon until he discovered Toby's body yesterday. Dawkin kept on saying "I see" although Will was not convinced that he believed a word of what Will was saying. His partner Sergeant Edgar took copious notes and manned the recording machine.

At the end, Dawkin thanked Will for his statement and said that he would be in touch soon.

Will arrived back from the police station having made his statement to the somewhat odious Dawkin and the house phone was ringing again. This time it was not Claire but another woman.

'Will, it's Sara.'

One of his Partners.

'Hi, Sara.'

'I tried your mobile several times but there is no reply. Are you OK?'

Will looked at his mobile and realised that it was out of juice.

'Yes, fine in the circumstances and I forgot to charge my phone.'

'We've heard the news. It's terrible. Must have been awful for you.'

'Yes, it was ghastly and I think the police think I killed him.'

'No, surely not.'

'Well, it is just my word as there were no other witnesses and they think I had a motive because of him and Claire. Anyway I will be back in the office tomorrow,' said Will.

'Will, that is why I am calling. We have had a few clients on the phone today asking about this and the three of us have had a meeting and think it is best if you take some leave until the situation is clearer.'

'What! That is ridiculous! It sounds as if you all think I did it.'

'Of course we don't, but we are concerned about the press and the reputation of the firm. Anyway, I am sorry Will but that is our decision. As you know, we act for a lot of high profile clients and we can't take the risk that this bad publicity will upset them. You must understand that.'

Will was silent for a while.

'Are you still there?' asked Sara.

'Yes, I was thinking. I believe you are all overreacting but I will abide by your decision for the time being.'

'Thank you, Will. I am sure it will be only for a short time until all the publicity dies down. Keep us in the picture. Take care and we will speak soon.'

'OK, will do,' replied Will without any enthusiasm.

'Bye, Will.'

Will put the phone down, walked into the lounge and slumped into a chair. In 48 hours his world had fallen apart. He was now a suspected murderer and unable to work. He wasn't sure what he should do. The whole situation was totally out of his control which was an experience that Will was not used to.

He poured himself a whisky and thought about what had happened. Who would have killed Toby and why? He imagined that some of Toby's business associates might be tough and he could imagine some of his deals might be "near the mark" but surely he had not involved himself in something that caused his death. And who were the two men who arrived so quickly at the scene? There was nothing Will could do to answer the questions which was so frustrating.

The house phone rang again, which reminded Will that he had to charge his mobile phone.

'Hello,' answered Will.

'Will, it is Michael Bore. I phoned the office and they said that you were having a break. As there was no reply on your mobile, I called home, hope that was OK?'

'Yes, no problem, Michael, but I am afraid I can't do anything for you. You may have heard but I am a suspect in a murder investigation and the office feels that I should take a break until all the publicity has died down. Why don't you have a chat with Sam or George, I am sure they could help you.'

'That's fine, Will, I heard but I was concerned for you and wondered if there was anything I could do to help?'

'That is kind of you Michael but I don't think there is anything anyone can do to help. I will have to wait until the police have done their work and find the killer. Until then, I seem to be in limbo.'

'Why don't you take a holiday? My villa in Mallorca is always available and actually I haven't been down for quite a while and wouldn't mind a friend taking a look around to make sure everything is shipshape. Check the security, that sort of thing. You can't always believe the agents.'

'Well, I don't know, I think I should probably stay here in case there is any news. In any case I doubt that the police would let me leave the country.'

'Have they taken your passport away?' asked Bore.

'No, but,' protested Will.

'Well, there you are. Ask them, I really could do with someone taking a look and think you could do with the break. I will get the boat stocked up too if you want to take a run in her.'

'OK, let me have a think and will get back to you. Thanks Michael.'

Will poured himself another whisky. What was he going to do? He hadn't had a holiday all summer and he could do with a few days away. He picked up the phone and dialled the number Inspector Dawkin had given him. Will thought Dawkin would still be working at six.

'Dawkin,' the Inspector said brusquely down the phone.

'Inspector, Will Slater here.'

'Ah, Mr Slater, have you remembered something or phoned to confess?' Dawkin said in an amused tone.

'No,' said Will, ignoring Dawkin's cheap comment. 'I wondered if you would have any problems if I had a few days in Mallorca, part-business and part-holiday.'

'Umm, not sure, it is not normal to let the main suspect in a murder enquiry leave the country.'

'But I am not really a suspect, just a witness, you know that,' said Will.

'Well, that's your interpretation, not necessarily mine. How long will you be gone for?'

'I don't know, say five days, perhaps a week. I will let you know where I am whenever you like. I am not going to run away and you haven't arrested me.'

'Not yet. OK, but I want you to phone me every other day or I will get the local police to arrest you. Please e-mail me your address on the island.'

'Agreed and thank you, Inspector.'

Will dialled Michael Bore.

'Michael, the police are happy for me to go so I think I will take you up on your offer.'

'Excellent, I will make sure the agents open up the villa and put in some provisions. Let me know what you find when you get there. Have a good trip. Speak soon.'

Will booked an open return ticket with BA, e-mailed the address of the villa to Dawkin and packed a small bag.

Chapter Eleven

Will flew to Palma, the capital of Mallorca. Although Will had been to Mallorca a few times, it had always been with Michael Bore, as this time he was alone, he thought he would search the Island on Wikipedia to see if there was anything interesting that he should look out for.

The entry said: *Mallorca, pronounced Majorca, is one of Spain's Balearic Islands in the Mediterranean. It's known for beach resorts, sheltered coves, limestone mountains and Roman and Moorish remains. Palma has most of the nightlife, the Moorish Almudaina royal palace and 13th-century Santa María Cathedral. Stone-built villages include Pollença, with its art galleries and music festival, and hillside Fornalutx, surrounded by citrus plantations.*

Will had always been surprised that the rich and famous built their villas in Mallorca as, when Will was growing up this was always seen to be a place of parties, cheap booze and vomit on the pavements. Although he understood there were parts of Mallorca that still attracted the "wrong type", from what he had seen, most of the Island was stunningly beautiful.

As the plane came into land, Will peered out of the window to see if he could see the famous Gothic Cathedral – La Seu – as they came into land at Son Sant Joan Airport.

From the airport, Will picked up a hire car and headed towards the villa which was situated between Pollenca and Puerto Pollenca on the north of the island. Michael Bore's villa was built into the hillside overlooking the port of Pollenca.

Will picked up the MA 13 motorway and head northeast across the island, passing through Inca and then tuning north towards Pollenca.

Will arrived at the villa and parked in the drive. The drive, big enough for four or five cars, was shaded by tall pine trees, a characteristic of the area. A different heat greeted Will from his air-conditioned car; delightfully warm air, tempered with a slight sea breeze. However, it was the smell that he noticed most, the scent of summer flowers and shrubs, hibiscus, bougainvillea and jasmine made a heady mix of sweet smells swirling on the breeze. He noticed that the lemon trees were laden with their fruit and knew that in the evening the mimosa tree would take over the mantle of providing the sweet aromas.

The front of the villa didn't look very spectacular, looking like a single story whitewashed building with red brick ridged tiles. However, this denied the reality that became obvious once inside.

The front door was typically Spanish, a thick wooded brown door with heavy architrave and the key, as always, was hidden in a secret compartment in the porch that could not be seen unless you knew where it was.

The villa was slightly convex in shape and built on two stories down the hillside. The living accommodation was on the ground floor and all the bedrooms were built on the floor below.

The front door opened up onto a huge lounge and dining area, red tiled floor and Moroccan rugs strategically scattered around. In the middle of the room was a wood burning stove for the colder Mallorcan evenings. To the right were the stairs down to the bedrooms, various cupboards and the guest toilet. To the left was a large modern kitchen. However, the focus of the room was the expansive view of Puerto Pollenca and the deep blue Mediterranean Sea, which could be seen from the floor to ceiling windows covering the whole width of the rear wall. The windows were in fact all glass doors that concertinaed back to allow access to the terrace with it views. The villa had been gently sculptured down the hillside on wide terraces. Below the main lounge terrace were the patios areas for each of the five large bedrooms and below that was another terrace housing the large eternity swimming pool and below that a well maintained and mature garden, with a lawn and borders, filled with agapanthus, angel trumpets, bird of paradise and hibiscus scrubs, that gently sloped down to the edge of the plot. Shady resting areas were everywhere to protect the guests from the searing summer heat provided by either the eponymous pines or graceful man built structures.

However, wherever you looked at the beauty of the design of the villa and the gardens, it was the breath-taking view that drew one's attention.

Will opened one of the glass doors and stepped onto the terrace and took in the smells and the view. It really was beautiful, over the tops of the pines Will could see the port; its boats with the sun glinting on the glass; to the right, the beach and beyond the blue water of the Mediterranean Sea. Perhaps, he was going to enjoy these few days more than he had thought.

Will took his bag downstairs and decided to have the middle of the five bedrooms. For no other reason than it was probably the biggest and the one Michael Bore used when he stayed. The room had that Spanish smell of wood furniture polish with a hint of cleaning material and mosquito repellent. The en-suite bathroom was large with everything one would have required including a built-in media system attached to one wall.

Will threw his bag onto the bed, removed his swimming trunks, picked up a large beach towel from the blanket box at the foot of the bed and armed with his sunscreen headed off to the beach.

Chapter Twelve

Will ate lunch at one of the beach restaurants, ordering the local grilled sardines, washed down with a couple of bottles of San Miguel beer. After lunch, he found a beach bed near to the water's edge and lay down to catch some of the late afternoon sun. The light warm breeze gently caressed Will's body, the smell of salt and seaweed, the sound of the waves lapping against the beach and the cacophony of children's voices squealing with delight in the gentle surf filled all his senses and he drifted off to sleep. When he woke, he swam and then made his way back to the villa.

Will showered in the luxurious bathroom and after he dressed, he thought that he should do the villa check as Michael Bore had asked, before he went out for dinner. He started in the bedrooms and generally checked that everything looked clean and all the bulbs worked. He also checked the patio doors and was surprised to find that the end bedroom patio door was unlocked. In an area where petty burglary was rife this seemed a serious error by the cleaners.

Will continued his check upstairs. On a table in the hall, Michael Bore had placed a visitors' book. Will always thought this strange as Michael never rented out the villa and it seemed that all it did was play to Michael's ego as guests wrote laudatory comments. Will picked it up and flicked through some of the pages. He was surprised to see that his partner, George Wright, had stayed a year or so ago. Will thought for a while and remembered that George had done some work for Michael and had been invited to stay over a weekend as a "thank you" for a job well done. Will put the book down, walked into the kitchen, took ice and tonic from the fridge and poured himself a gin and tonic. He took his drink out to the veranda and spent the next twenty minutes staring at the view.

After checking that the villa was locked and secure, Will walked up the hill into Pollenca. He planned to have dinner at Michael's favourite fish restaurant on the edge of the main square.

Many of the houses in Pollenca were built in the 17th and 18th centuries and many streets were very narrow and compact, a legacy from the medieval era. The central square, called Plaça Major, where Will was going to eat was dominated by a large 13th-century church "Our Lady of the Angels" which was built by the Knights Templar.

One of the town's most distinctive features was the 365-step stairway north of the square; this led up to a chapel on top of the hill known as Calvary. On Good Friday, this was the setting for the most dramatic parade of the year. On the road winding up the back of the hill, there was a re-enactment of the Stations of the Cross. This was followed by a mock crucifixion on top of the hill after which the figure of Christ was ceremonially removed from the Cross. There was a sombre, torch-lit parading of the body of Christ through the town led by hundreds of people in cloaks, masks and pointed hats and done in total silence, save for the slow beating of a drum.

Will was just looking at the miniature fishing boat filled with ice and the fish catch of the day outside the restaurant when the owner appeared at the door.

'Señor Slater, how good to see you. You are well?'

'Yes, very well, Manual and you?'

'Ah, you know,' he said raising his shoulders and holding out his hands, 'business could be better. The government doesn't understand small businesses like mine.'

The world over, thought Will.

'And how is Señor Bore? Is he with you?' he asked looking over Will's shoulder inquiringly.

'No, I have come alone for a few days this time.'

'You come in and I choose some good fish for you. You go to the opera in the square after?'

'I didn't know there was one. What are they singing?'

'Ah, Cossi Fan Tutte, one of my favourites. You go get a ticket while I pour you a glass of Rioja,' said Manuel indicating in the general direction of the square outside.

After dinner Will settled into his seat to listen to the stage version of the opera, relaxing in the warm evening air.

He might not have been so relaxed if he had seen the man standing in the shadows to one side of the square paying particular attention to him.

Will read through the programme notes.

Cossi Fan Tutte, translated as 'Thus do they all' was written by Wolfgang Amadeus Mozart and first performed in 1790 in Vienna.

Will reminded himself of the synopsis and in modern parlance, the opera would have been described as a romantic comedy.

The performance didn't end until after midnight and Will was feeling pretty tired by the time he had walked back to the villa. He had forgotten to turn on any lights when he left earlier so everything was in darkness when he entered the villa. He found the alarm and turned it off and switched on some lights. For some reason he stood and listened for a few moments but heard nothing. He left a light on in the main living room and went straight to his room. He undressed, cleaned his teeth and was asleep in minutes.

Will woke up unsure for a moment where he was, what time it was and what had woken him but was sure the noise was unnatural. He lay there listening, unused to the inherent noises of the villa. He could hear the gentle tapping of the bougainvillea against the windows in the night breeze but that was not what had woken him. Then he heard it again, it was the sound of someone trying to open the patio doors. The hairs stood up on the back of Will's arms. He got out of bed and called out.

'Who's there?'

The patio light switch was on the other side of the room but for some reason he didn't want to walk across the room and stayed tucked into the wall beside the bathroom door. It was good intuition as two bullets sprayed through the glass patio doors.

Will hit the floor but knew he had to get out before the glass shattered and whoever was out there got in. The bedroom door was close to where he lay so he part slid and part commando crawled to the door. He reached up and opened the door and was now in the corridor which accessed all the rooms. He decided to rush for the stairs as more shots rained through the patio doors. Once upstairs he push the panic button on the alarm and was greeted by a shrill piercing sound and hoped that whoever was on the other end was as vigilant as the time he burned the bacon which set off the fire alarm. A voice came from the alarm box, which made Will jump. Something mumbled in Spanish.

'*Policía. Urgente. Policía*,' shouted Will.

'OK, OK' came back the voice.

Will wasn't sure how long they would take but ran into the kitchen, picked up a large knife and decided the best place to hide was in the guest toilet.

He ran across the living room to the toilet, locked the door and wedged a small chair under the door handle to stop it being opened. The toilet had an angled wall to make room for the cupboard next to it and therefore he could hide out of line from any bullets shot directly through the door.

He thought several times that he could hear footsteps on the tiled floor outside but the alarm was loud and he could not be sure.

In the distance, Will heard the sirens. It sounded as if there was more than one vehicle approaching.

Will now wished he had opened the front door as the police would not be able to get in. Perhaps, he could sneak out open it and hide again. He listened to see if he could hear anyone outside.

Will was a devotee of crime and adventures novels and had read in many of them that one never stands where an attacker is expecting you, so Will quietly removed the chair, unlocked the door and, crouching on his knees, reached up turned the door handle and pulled the door open towards him. As the door swung open, Will saw a pair of legs immediately outside the door in front of him. Will looked up and the killer had his gun pointed straight ahead and not at Will's level. In that instant, Will drove the kitchen knife through the killer's foot, slammed the door closed, wedging the chair under the handle again and rolled to cover beside the door. He heard the killer cursing and then two shots were fired through the door.

The sirens were very loud now and he hoped this would frighten the killer and he would run. Will waited and then he heard loud banging on the front door.

It was time to try and make a break for it. Will opened the toilet door again, once again keeping very low and to his relief there were no legs outside the toilet just some drops of blood, still keeping low he raced the few meters to the front door and swung it open to be faced by three Spanish policemen all pointing their carbines at him.

Will cried 'Help!' hoping this would demonstrate him as the victim as opposed to the perpetrator. From behind the policemen appeared a representative from the alarm company and whose English was good and Will explained what had happen.

The killer must have pulled the knife from his foot and flung it in the living room as it lay on one of the Moroccan rugs and there was a trail of blood leading down the stairs. Two of the policemen rushed off in pursuit of the attacker following the blood trail.

Will sat down shaken and explained to the security representative the whole story.

After a few minutes, one of the policemen came back and had an animated conversation in Spanish with the security man. When they had finished the security man informed Will that his assailant was dead.

'Killed by the police?' exclaimed Will.

'No, they have found him dead by the pool. He appears to have slipped, perhaps on his own blood and cracked his head on a rock along one of the flower beds!'

Will's initial reaction was relief but realised that he might now be suspected of this man's killing too. It was only his word.

'The police want you to go to the police headquarters in town to make a statement,' the security man informed him.

Will got dressed and as the police led Will out to their car, he noticed another car parked close up to the side door of the villa that had not been there when he had got back last night. He was going to make some comment but the security man had got back into his car and it was obvious that the policemen spoke very little English. He assumed it must be the attacker's car and he would mention it later.

Two hours later, after taking his statement and as the sun was rising, the security representative dropped Will back at the villa. He noticed that the other car had gone so assumed the police had taken it away for forensics so made no mention of it.

Apparently, the Spanish equivalent of SOCO had all left and the drive was empty of all vehicles apart from Will's hire car.

The security representative asked if Will would be staying in the villa. Will looked at his watch, it was now 6 a.m. he was certainly not spending any more time here and the security man agreed to wait while Will re-packed his bag. The security man agreed to tell the agent to clean the villa and repair the damage. Will made a mental note to call Michael later in the morning to tell him what had happened.

Chapter Thirteen

Will drove his car down to the port and into the large car park which was situated immediately behind a row of shops, restaurants and businesses that overlooked the promenade. He parked and sat on a bench and watched for ten minutes to see if anyone had followed him. Satisfied, he went back to his car, got in the back and promptly slept for the next three hours.

When he woke, the port was in full swing and the car park was busy. Will was still in shock from last night's events and didn't think he could drive to the airport to re-arrange his flights, so he decided he would rest on Michael's boat for a few hours until he felt stronger. Will picked up his small bag from the car boot and walked around to a shop that sold all manner of nautical wares and acted as an agent and chandler for many of the boats moored in the harbour including Michael Bore's.

As Will approached the front of the building, he had obviously been spotted from inside as a large rotund man rushed out and clasped Will in a bear hug.

'Señor Slater, good to see you.'

'Good to see you too, Senor Sanchez.'

'Señor Bore said you might come, everything is ready and as you British say "shipshape".' He then exploded into a quivering mass as he laughed at his joke.

'I have the keys for the boat, wait.' Sanchez then disappeared back into his shop and a minute or so later reappeared with a small key fob with a number of keys.

'You know which is which, one for the storage cupboards, one for the cabin door and one for the engine start,' he said as he flicked each key on the ring.

'Many thanks, Señor Sanchez. I am not proposing to take the boat out of the harbour, I am just going to use it to rest for a while.'

Sanchez shrugged and repeated that it was all ready if he wanted. They shook hands and Will headed for the entrance to the port. He crossed the promenade, to his right the road made its way along the beachfront and to the left, the road meandered under a canopy of pine trees shading some expensive beachfront properties.

The promenade had a smattering of patrons, drinking their first coffees of the morning or eating their breakfast. He noticed a blackboard in front of one of the small restaurants advertising a "full English breakfast" and Will wondered if this was, in fact, the best British brand that had been exported across the world.

The port consisted of a number of pontoons that ran out into the sea, with the boats moored either side of each pontoon. The entrance to the pontoons was via a Perspex door with a key pad to stop unauthorised visitors having access to the expensive pieces of hardware beyond. Will used the key fob to open the door. Avenues of blue and white representing millions of pounds, stretched before him. Michael Bore's boat was in the middle pontoon. The sun shone brightly now from a cloudless sky and reflected off the aluminium and the highly polished fibreglass of the boats. The spinnakers were fluttering in the breeze and their tinkling challenged the seagulls' airtime.

Michael's boat, however, was the ugly duckling. It was certainly not all shining and gleaming as it was a converted wooded and steel workboat which was a dirty brown amongst the blues and the whites. But it had a charm and as one would expect, it had been converted to a high level of comfort whilst maintaining its working vessel's appearance. Michael had named the boat "Bruno". Will was not sure where the name came from as Michael Bore wasn't a dog fan, as far as he knew. Michael had always said it was a lucky family name. But the name fitted the boat especially well amongst it sleeker and more lady-like companions.

Will clambered onto the deck of the boat which was most of its aft. This was where a working crane had been sited and you could see the replacement planks where the fixtures for the crane had been removed from the deck. The whole deck was now highly polished and was the outdoor living space of the boat. Built all around the deck sides were low storage units.

The original steel wire rails around the deck, to prevent anyone from falling overboard, had been replace by teak balustrades, so the storage units acted as seating too. The unit nearest to the cabin was a large cool box well stocked with beers, white wine and champagne. Another unit had snorkelling and scuba kit, another had folding deck tables and chairs and another had collapsible loungers and mattresses. Towards the aft were two steel cups sunk into the deck. These were for housing two metal poles which provided the attachment for the sun awning that could be reeled out from the top of the wheelhouse to provide shelter from the sun for the whole deck.

The wheelhouse had been completely changed. The rear wall remained and had the fixture for the awning but was now made of a non-reflective see-through material so whoever was driving could see and communicate with those on the deck. A new driving seat had been placed at a higher level so the driver could see above the cabin roof with another awning for protection from the sun.

The cabin was entered from a door to the right of the steering seat down a few stairs and had also been completely modernised. There was a modern galley and seating area in the aft of the cabin and then two double sleeping berths on either side of the boat and a lavatory and wet room shower in the forward of the boat. The berths unlike many modern yachts were not the typical envelopes which challenged even those without claustrophobia but were full head height and had an airy feel.

Will dropped his bag on one of the double beds and headed to the wet room for a shower.

Chapter Fourteen

Will sat in a deckchair browsing at a newspaper he had picked up at the chandler's store. He closed his eyes and let the warm sunshine soak through him but he couldn't stop thinking about how his personal circumstances had changed over the last two weeks. From a peaceful and contented existence to one of violence and fear. He remembered that he needed to ring Dawkin as he had promised.

Will glanced down at the paper again when he saw a movement from the corner of his eye. He looked up and saw a woman at the far end of the pontoon. She looked from side to side at the boats as if trying to locate a particular one. She carried a small bag in her hand and had a couple of shoulder bags. She was wearing cut-off jeans and a T-shirt and Will thought she would certainly look the part on one of the surrounding gin palaces. As she approached he looked back at his paper so as not to stare.

'Mr Slater?' the woman asked standing on the pontoon at the aft of Bruno.

Will looked up surprised that she had stopped at his boat.

'Yes,' replied Will.

'My name is Jay Encort, Señor Sanchez said I could find you here and thought you might help me?' she paused. 'I am a freelance photographer and have an assignment for a UK Sunday paper to do some shots of the Mallorcan coast but remote spots taken from the sea. No one will let me hire a boat by myself due to the danger from the rocks around the coast and there is no one around to take me out. Señor Sanchez thought you would consider it?'

'I am sorry, but I am only here for a short time and was not planning to move the boat,' replied Will.

'I can pay for the fuel and your time if you want, it is very important to me.'

Will smiled and shook his head.

'That's not the issue,' he said.

By now Jay had taken off her shoulder bags, which Will assumed contained her camera equipment, and stood there with appealing eyes.

For some reason Will found himself saying 'OK' as in truth he could do with some company and it might be safer at sea than in the harbour.

Jay was already wearing deck shoes and bounded aboard with all her gear.

'Thank you very much, that is brilliant,' she said as she shook Will's hand.

'There is an empty cabin on the right, put your gear in there and we can go,' said Will settling into the idea of a trip to sea.

Will watched Jay disappear below and thought perhaps he would delay his journey home and it might be a pleasant few days after all.

Jay appeared back after a few minutes in a bikini top, her cut-off jeans and panoply of camera kit strung across her shoulder.

She was probably in her late thirties, short brown hair, that looked practical to maintain and an attractive face. She was about 5'8" tall and looked as if she worked out regularly in a gym. There was just the hint of a "six pack" in her abdomen and her legs and arms looked muscular. Will thought it must be because of heaving all that camera equipment about.

'I usually have the owner with me when we sail this boat, so excuse me if I look a bit uncoordinated,' said Will.

Will cast off the moorings, aft from the pontoon and forward from the boat next to it.

Will sat in the driver's seat started the engines and raised the anchor. Carefully, he maneuvered the boat out of the port and into the beautifully blue waters of the Mediterranean Sea.

Chapter Fifteen

Will steered the boat first eastward to navigate the Cap
Formentor peninsula before swinging around and sailing
westwards along the northern coast of the Island towards Calle
Sant Vicent and further east. The northern coast of Mallorca
was much rockier and the less accessible part of the coast and
therefore less photographed with unoccupied beaches and
coves. Jay spent the morning moving up and down the side of
the boat taking pictures at various angles. Occasionally, asking
Will to let the boat drift to get a stiller picture.

Will was enjoying himself, the sky was blue as was the sea
and Jay was very pleasant company.

At lunchtime, they moored and Jay thought they should
swim, removing her shorts and promptly diving into the sea.
Will let out the rope ladder over the side of the boat so they
could get back in again and dove off the side too. The water
was deep so it felt cold but after a few strokes Will was warm
and followed after Jay who was swimming for the nearest
beach. When Will arrived on the beach Jay was lying on the
wet sand, eyes closed, absorbing the warm sunshine.

'What a beautiful spot this is,' she said as Will, breathing
heavily, sat down beside her.

'I doubt many people have ever been on this beach,' said
Will looking up at the cliffs surrounding the cove and noting
there appeared to be no way down from the top.

'Right,' said Jay, 'race you back to the boat for lunch.'

And with that she was up and back in the water. Will had
little doubt who would win the race but made an effort to look
as if he had accepted the challenge.

When eventually he arrived and clambered up the ladder he
was puffing considerably. On the other hand, Jay stood with her

arms on her hips looking as if she had been standing there the whole time.

'I think we know who won that race,' she said laughing.

'No doubt about that,' said Will bending over trying to get his breath back and laughing, too.

Will placed the awning poles into their holders in the deck and rolled out the deck canopy. They ate bread and local cheese and drank cold beer for lunch.

Jay explained during lunch that her name was really Josephine but her younger brother couldn't pronounce the name when he was young and shortened it to "J", which stuck. She was a single parent with a twelve-year-old daughter who lived with her parents for continuity purposes because as a photographer she travelled a lot. Her husband, a soldier, had been killed in Iraq and since then she was the family's breadwinner. Each weekend she stayed with her daughter and parents, unless she was out of the country. It appeared to Will that Jay was really quite lonely even though she seemed to lead a busy life.

After lunch they cruised further around the island further until they reached the place where Will had decided to moor up for the night. He had settled on this spot as there was an excellent restaurant at the top of the cliff that could be accessed seaward via a stone staircase that ran into the sea. The only difficulty was that the mooring was in a relatively narrow channel between two ridges of submerged rocks. These were clearly marked by buoys but even so, Will took the boat into the channel very slowly and let the anchors down.

After they had showered, Will let down the tender boat from its harness and motored out to the bottom of the stone staircase. The tide was in, so he left a long lead on the mooring rope as the tide would go out whilst they ate.

The restaurant was perched right on the cliff edge and the rear patio eating area was shaded by pine trees. The tables were covered in pink table clothes, every table was positioned so it had an uninterrupted and spectacular view of the Mediterranean Sea. They ate soft shell crabs and monkfish and drank Chablis as they watched a cruise ship move between the islands and numerous small fishing boats heading back to port. The sea was calm with the early evening sun reflecting off the waves. The seagulls caught the reflection of the setting sun and looked like bright lights skirting across the sky; the clouds turned pink from the same reflection and matched the colour of the table clothes.

Will and Jay talked more about their backgrounds, their work and their children as they finished off a second bottle of wine.

After dinner, the walk down the stone staircase to the tender was precarious, not just because of the wine but the tide's newly exposed steps were covered with seaweed and green slime and were extremely slippery.

Will moored the tender to the aft of Bruno and helped Jay on board. As Will was just boarding from the tender, the boat rocked from a swell and Jay steadied Will to avoid him going overboard. They stood facing each other very close and Jay gently kissed Will on the lips.

Will was not sure what was going to happen next or what he should do, as he had not been in a situation like this for a long time.

Jay reached up behind her, and with one hand, undid the knot in her halter neck dress and let it drop to the deck revealing that she was naked underneath, apart from a thong. Although Will had seen Jay in a bikini, seeing her with virtually nothing on was different. Her body was well muscled and her breasts were small, up-turned with large nipples. They reminded Will of schoolboys' drawings.

Jay stepped delicately out of her dress and picked it up, took Will's hand and led him to the cabin.

Will was now in no doubt as to what was going to happen next or what he was supposed to do.

Chapter Sixteen

Will woke and lay in the bed listening to the sounds made by a boat moored at anchor. The gentle lapping of the water against the hull, the creaking of the vessel pulling against its anchors and the sound of seagulls searching for their breakfast. He looked across at Jay who was sound asleep. Her back was bear and he could just see the start of the upward curve of her buttocks and he felt himself stirring again. He needed a pee first and pulled on a pair of shorts and headed towards the deck. Normally, he would have not have peed over the side but for some reason on that morning he did.

The sun was barely visible above the horizon and when he finished he looked out to sea drinking in the clear fresh morning air and anticipating the next few minutes with Jay.

As Will turned to go below deck something caught the corner of his eye. He looked again and noticed a boat out at sea. It looked strange. He reached into the cabin and took a pair of binoculars from a hook in the doorway and focused on the distant boat. It appeared to be drifting and its mast seemed to be lying partly over the hull. He could see a couple of people on the boat and they, having spotted him, were waving.

He would have to tow the distressed boat into port, this was the unwritten behaviour at sea. The current seemed to be stronger further out from the protection of the bay as the distressed boat was moving reasonably quickly. He was just about to hang the binoculars back on their hook, before waking up Jay and starting up the motors to carry out the rescue mission, when something made him look again at the troubled boat. He looked closely at the boat from forward to aft and then he saw them. Bubbles in the water from the aft of the boat. It was under motor so not in distress.

Will dashed below and called to Jay.

'Get up quickly, we have to move, we are under attack from pirates.'

Will ran back to the deck and started the engines and pulled up the anchors. Jay arrived on deck seconds later.

'You will need to steer,' shouted Will. 'Head for those two buoys at the end of the channel as fast as you can. We have to get there and into open waters before the pirates can cut us off.'

Jay sat in the driver's seat and pulled down the engine throttle lever increasing the speed of the boat until the Paxman diesels were at their maximum revolutions.

'Surely, pirates don't exist anymore,' called out Jay.

'They exist all around the world. They are the modern day sea equivalent of burglars and bank robbers, but even worse as they often rape their victims and then kill them afterwards,' replied Will.

'Ooo,' replied Jay.

Will used the on-board radio and called mayday. A voice answered in Spanish and when Will started speaking in English the dispatcher changed to English, too.

'We are being attacked by pirates,' shouted Will into the receiver.

'What is your location?' came back the dispatcher.

Will read out the location coordinates from the on on-board equipment.

'We are sending out the Coastguard immediately. Do not engage with the pirates.'

Fat chance, Will thought.

Will rushed below deck again and opened the first bench cupboard in the cabin. He threw out the spare bed sheets and other linen and opened a compartment at the bottom. There lay a sawn off shotgun and a box of cartridges. Michael had always told Will that the sea was a dangerous place and one should be prepared for all eventualities.

Will picked up the gun and grabbed a handful of cartridges and shoved them in the pocket of his shorts.

He went back on deck and noticed that the Bruno was not moving as quickly as it should and then realised the tender was being dragged along behind. It could not be stowed on board while the boat was in motion so he went below into the cabin again and this time came back with a large carving knife from the galley and raced to the stern of the boat and started hacking at the mooring rope. It took him a good two minutes and then the rope sheered and the tender was cut loose. Michael would not be pleased to see the £2,000 bit of kit cast aside but Will noticed the boat pick up speed immediately. He moved back to the cabin where Jay was doing a good job in keeping the boat in the channel but the pirates seemed to be getting nearing and looked as if they would reach the end of the channel before the Bruno. The pirates had pulled their sail on board and were making better progress. Will needed to slow them down and called out that if they did not alter course, he would fire on them. Whether they heard or even understood was not clear but it made no difference and Will decided to fire a couple of gunshot rounds above their heads. He could now see their faces and there was a grim determination on their swarthy features. Will reloaded both barrels of the gun and fired again over the pirates heads. This time Will shots were matched with a couple of rounds in return which sent both Will and Jay diving to the deck. Jay was up in no time and keeping her head low managed to keep the boat on position in the channel. Will had an idea and went below again. This time he returned with the flare gun. Taking careful aim and keeping his head just above the bulwark, he fired it into the pirates' boat. For a few moments nothing happened but then a dull glow appeared as the flare must have buried itself amongst the debris of the sail and mast lying on the deck. Then there was a small explosion and the sail burst into flames. It was the distraction that Will needed, the pirate boat went off course and slowed down as the pirates tried to put out the fire.

Bruno reached the end of the channel and out safely into open water.

Will called "Mayday" again and got the same dispatcher and gave them the new coordinates and explained that they were heading west around the island.

After about 10 minutes a sleek and fast-looking boat appeared from the east heading in their direction. When it saw Bruno, it steered towards them. It was the Coastguards. Will shouted across to them explaining where the pirates were and that their boat was on fire. He also mentioned that they had lost their tender and if they found it, could they tow it into the port.

With a shrug of the shoulders, the Coastguard skipper gave an instruction to the coxswain of the boat and it moved off at speed in the direction Will had given.

Both Jay and Will were shocked by the whole experience although Will did notice that Jay seemed to have coped very well under the pressure of gunfire and seemed to get over the bad experience quicker than Will.

They decided to give the scene of the incident a wide berth and turned off the engines and drifted while they rested.

Will thought it was time to explain to Jay what had happened to him over the last two weeks and that in the last 24 hours his life had been in danger twice. Jay listened intently to the story, nodding and murmuring at the appropriate times. But again Will thought she was less horrified than he would have been, had it been the other way around. She was obviously made of sterner stuff!

They headed back to the port but decided it was too dangerous to stay on board and needed to move to a hotel. They could have gone to the Formentor Hotel, one of an international chain, but opted for the family run hotel immediately opposite the beach.

The hotel was whitewashed with green shutters and Will and Jay had a large double room with air conditioning and a balcony overlooking the beach.

It was not long before the memories of the night before overtook the stress of the day and they ended back in bed. This time their lovemaking was slower and more satisfying.

They spent the next three days making love, eating out at the various restaurants along the marina and discussing Will's circumstances. Will also remembered to phone both Dawkin, who seemed totally uninterested in his location or predicament and Michael Bore, who seemed somewhat agitated by what he heard.

Jay seemed very interested in Will's predicament and offered various scenarios as to the chain of events that occurred. As often as they talked about it, they could not draw any links between Toby's death, the attack at the villa and the pirates. Although they both agreed there had to be some link.

Chapter Seventeen

Jay and Will booked flights back on the same plane and arrived back to a wet and cold Gatwick. They took the Gatwick Express into Paddington Station and after a long and slow kiss goodbye, went their separate ways to their own homes promising to phone each other that evening.

Will arrived back at his Wimbledon home flinging his bag down in the hall and immediately poured himself a large whisky which he took into the conservatory to ponder on the events of the last week. What was there left to consider? He was not used to this, after all he was a commercial lawyer, not some spook, but he could not shake off the feeling that he had to come up with the answers and who was to say that there would not be a third attempt on his life. He shuddered and got up and checked all the windows and doors to make sure they were securely locked.

He poured himself another drink and closed his eyes. What was he missing? It had all started with the call from Toby. Perhaps there was clue in the house in the Highlands. He could not go back to work so perhaps another visit to Ballachulish might provide an answer.

He phoned Jay and after telling her how much he enjoyed her company and hoped to see a lot more of her, he explained that he was going to Scotland the next day to see if he could find anything out from Toby's house. Jay told him to be careful. He said he would.

Will rose early the next day and was on the 9 a.m. flight to Glasgow. However, the weather in Scotland had taken a turn for the worse and the sky was overcast with a menacing look to it.

The same car hire receptionist, from his last visit, greeted Will and suggested that he needed a different type of vehicle this time as the forecast was for snow. He suggested an all-wheel drive Subaru.

The drive out of Glasgow was uneventful but as soon as he reached Loch Lomond the snow started falling. The traffic kept the road clear but the snow was heavy and was lying at the side of the road. As he got into the town of Tydrum, Will joined a line of traffic that has been stopped by the police. A policeman was walking down the line of vehicles and speaking to each driver in turn.

When the policeman got to Will's car, he gestured with his hand for Will to wind down his window.

'Where are you going, sir?' asked the policeman.

'Up to Ballachulish, officer,' Will replied.

'The weather is getting worse, sir, and we are about to close the road,' said the policeman.

'It is very important that I get there as have just come up from London for a meeting and I purposely got a 4-wheel drive car.'

The policeman looked up the line of vehicles and turned back to Will.

'OK, you see that logging lorry?' pointed the policeman. Will craned his neck out of the window.

'The one with all the logs, five vehicles along the line,' indicated the policeman.

'Yes, I see it,' said Will.

'It is going up to the saw mill at Fort William, as soon as you see it leave, pull in behind and it will keep the road clear and you should be able to follow it as far as Ballachulish, although I am not sure how you will get back. So my advice would be not to start.'

'OK, thanks officer, I do need to go, I will stay at the hotel in Ballachulish until I can get back.'

'OK,' mumbled the policeman and walked on to the car behind.

Will closed his window and waited until the logging lorry decided to move on.

In the meantime, the policeman had moved down the line of vehicles and Will paid no attention to the black Range Rover which pulled out from the line of vehicles and drove on up the road towards Ballachulish and Fort William.

After about 10 minutes, the logging lorry indicated and pulled out of the line of vehicles and Will followed.

Will could see why the police were going to close the road, the snow was falling very heavily and the visibility was limited, but he tucked in behind the lorry as it cranked up through it gears and started the journey along the A82, which would lead through the Bridge of Orchy, across Rannock Moor and into the depth of Glencoe before it reached Ballachulish.

The lorry sped up as it had good traction on the road because of its weight and it was not long before the lorry had opened up a gap between the two vehicles. Will concentrated on keeping the lorry's lights in sight rather than trying to catch up. The snow was so heavy that the lorry's tracks were being covered in the short distance between the two vehicles.

They passed the pub where Will had had the conversation with the local about the massacre at Glencoe and the road then snaked up over Rannock Moor to Glencoe. Everything was white or more accurately grey, Will now understood the use of the "white out" poles that he had noticed on his last trip and how essential they were. It was impossible to make out the side of the road as everything was the same colour, the near distance and the far distance. The windscreen wipers were struggling to clear the weight of the snow falling. One mistake and the car would be off the road and into one of the ditches that ran alongside.

Will had now lost sight of the lorry altogether and was just aiming the car to the right of the next white out pole to ensure he stayed on the road. There was nothing else he could do. He couldn't stop, he just had to hope that the Subaru with its 4-wheel drive would keep him going through the ever-increasing thickness of the snow on the road. Will now wished he had taken the policeman's advice and stayed in Tyndrum. But then, just as the steep climb into Glencoe had started, the clouds parted and there was bright sunshine with a blue sky. To Will's left there was still the floor to ceiling opaque covering of snow and cloud and to his right brightness. It was like someone opening a curtain very slowly. The snow was still thick but he could now make out the road and up ahead he could again see the logging lorry chugging its way up through the rock walls of Glencoe. If the road had been straighter, he would also have seen up ahead the black Range Rover also making its way laboriously through the snow.

The snow was lighter in the shadow of Glencoe and Will made better time as the road made its way down from the height of the mountain towards Loch Kinleven and Ballachulish.

Will arrived at the turnoff to Toby's house and noticed by the tracks running down the middle of the small lane that another vehicle had passed this way very recently. Whoever was in the other vehicle had gone past the gate to Toby's house as the snow was completely virgin as Will pulled in through the bar gate and pulled up outside the front door. He hoped that Toby's habit of a lifetime of leaving a key under the plant pot outside the house was unchanged, otherwise, Will would need to break in somehow.

As Will got out of the car, his foot hit a patch of ice under the snow and fell sideways into the snow just as he heard a crack and something bounce off the roof of the car. As Will struggled to get up on the slippery ground something hit the snow beside him and he realised that someone was shooting at him. He cowered down beside the car as two more shots rang out. Will estimated that the gunman was up on the bank on the opposite side of the road to the house directly in line with the front door. Will had stopped the car at an angle to the house so he could not reach either the pot where he had hoped the key would be hidden, or the front door without moving from the cover of the car and presenting a clear target for the gunman. Will needed to move the car so that it provided cover to the front door and the pot. The driver's door was still open from when he had slipped over. As Will moved his position so he could lean into the car from the ground, the shooter fired again and the bullet took out the passenger's window. Keeping low and reaching into the car Will was able to release the hand break and adjust the steering wheel so he could manoeuvre the car into a position to provide cover to the front door. Now, Will had to move the car which was not going to be easy in the thick snow. It then occurred to Will that the gunman could easily just climb down from the bank and shoot Will at close range. He put that thought out of his mind and started to rock the car back and forward although it was difficult to get much of a grip on the ground in a crouch position, he eventually got some momentum and the car crunched forward on the crisp snow a few inches. Will estimated he needed to move the car about three feet. He had to take a risk otherwise he was going to be trapped there. He dug his heels in the ground and lent back against the open driver's door and hoped his head was not too exposed to the gunman or that the gunman was not that good a marksman. Will pushed back with all his strength and for a few seconds the car stayed motionless then it seemed to shudder forward and Will almost lost his footing but he managed to keep his balance and give the car another shove and it started to move very slowly until it was now in the position Will wanted. Will heard another shot and ducked. It sounded different to the others but he was no expert. Keeping the car in line to where he estimated the gunman was, he scuttled on all fours to the pot and lifting it up, felt for a key. At first, he could not feel anything and then his fingers felt the hardness of a key. The next question was would the car still provide cover as he crawled to the front door? Was the shooter high enough to see over the car with an angle to enable him to get a clear shot? Now was the time to find out.

Will crawled towards the door and reached up to put the key in the lock and waited for the bullet to come.

Silence.

He turned the key and crawled in, slamming the door behind him. Will sat in the hall with his back to the door and panted from the stress.

Will thought that he had to arm himself in case the killer decided to enter the house. A knife from the kitchen would be no good against a gun. He needed one of Toby's guns.

Will walked across to the gun cabinet. Locked, as he had expected it to be. He didn't think he would be able to break the cabinet open. He peered at the lock. A small key was required. He wondered where he would find this. He then remembered the small key that was on the floor when he came last time. It was still on the shelf where he had left it. He tried it in the lock, it turned and the cupboard opened.

There were three guns in the cabinet, two shotguns and a .2 rifle. Will chose the shotgun. Underneath the cabinet was a drawer with boxes of shells. He loaded two into the gun and pocketed a handful. Will walked through into the kitchen and sat down and thought about what he should do next. Somehow, he thought, he needed to know who was trying to kill him as the next attempt might be successful. That meant he had to find the gunman first rather than the other way around. He had decided.

He removed his shoes and socks and put on a pair of wellington boots and some thick socks which were by the back door. He took a woollen hat hanging from a hook and pulled out the gloves from his pocket. He slipped the latch from the back door and walked out. He listened but heard nothing. He walked in a straight line keeping the house between him and the gunman. He let himself out of the garden gate at the end of the garden and walked about 50 yards directly south still with the house behind him. He then bared left towards the wood. The snow was deep and Will fell several times, falling over hummocks of grass covered by the deep snow. His feet were now very cold and his wellies full of snow. When he got to the wood, there was less snow and he was able to make better time. His plan was to cross the road further down from where he estimated the shooter was and approach him from behind.

Will reached the road and cautiously peered out. To his right was a small car tucked into the side of the road. It looked empty. He crossed the road quickly and tried the doors. All locked. He peered in but there seemed to be nothing visible. The bank behind the car looked steep so he walked further to his right until he found a spot where the roots of the tree provided a few steps and handholds to allow Will to clamber up. At the top of the bank, he continued with his plan to walk north and then arc back to approach the shooter from behind. Will continued moving north until he reached a fence. He then turned left and walked towards where the shooter was situated. As he got nearer, he slowed down and stopped and listened. He could hear nothing apart from his breathing. He crouched down and peered through the trees to see if he could see anything. He thought he could see a pair of legs. He moved slowly and as quietly as he could towards the legs. When he thought he was suitably near, he stood and called out.

'Put your gun down and stand up I am armed.'

There was no movement from the prone figure. Will shouted again.

'Get up and put your gun down.'

Still no movement. Will took a step forward and got a clear view of the shooter. He then noticed a patch of red in the snow beside the gunman. Will then noticed a wound in the back of the gunman's head. Will was in no doubt that the man was dead. Will kicked the man's foot but wasn't expecting any reaction. Will was relieved but realised that there was someone else out here too. He looked around, his breath steaming in the air. There were no sounds at all, even the birds were quiet. The blue sky had disappeared and was now grey again. He couldn't see any movement and everything seemed deadened from the snow lying on the ground. There was a menacing feel about the landscape. Will shivered but only partly from the cold that was seeping through his body. Will decided to head back to the house as quickly as possible.

Chapter Eighteen

Will slid down the bank on his bottom to get to the road. He walked briskly across the drive, keeping his gun pointed out in front of him and looking from side to side, towards the house. The snow was unspoiled so he knew that no one had walked this way. He opened the gate at the side of the house and walked towards the back door at the rear of the house.

As he turned, the corner of the house towards the back door, he could see the footprints he had made when he had left the house, but as he looked down at the snow, he saw with horror another pair of footprints coming from the opposite corner of the house. They stopped at the back door. There was now someone else in the house. Who? Will assumed the person who had killed the shooter was now waiting for him. Will had to make a decision. Either return to his car or challenge whoever was in the house. He had come up to Scotland to find more clues to resolve his situation so it seemed pointless to leave now.

Will opened the backdoor pushing it wide whilst standing in cover behind the back wall of the house. He called through the door.

'I know you are in there. I have got a gun and I will shoot you.'

Initially, Will heard nothing then a scuffling noise and the sound of what sounded like a window opening and then silence.

'I am coming in,' called Will and he stepped into the kitchen pointing the shotgun in front of him. He walked into the hall, no one there and he could feel cold air coming from the study on his right. With his heart beating loudly, he stepped through the door and noticed that the window was wide open. He did a quick sweep of the room with his eyes and stepped across to the window. He could see footprints outside the

71

window disappearing into the wood directly to the east of the house. Will watched but could not see anyone. A couple of moments later, as he peered through the window, he saw a black Range Rover move down the road towards Ballachulish.

Will closed the window and looked around him. The room had been ransacked, papers scattered everywhere. Someone was looking for something and Will didn't know whether they had been successful. Will did a search of the rest of the house to make sure he was alone, but the house had that empty feel. He made his way back into the kitchen and locked the back door. He removed his willies, the sodden socks and dried his feet on a kitchen towel. He put on his own socks and shoes and went back into the study and sat down with the shotgun across his knees.

What was the intruder looking for? Will looked around the room scanning the papers scattered on the floor and then his eyes caught a name he recognised amongst the papers. He bent down and picked up a blank piece of headed notepaper with the name "Java PLC". The same name as the file that Will had found tucked into George Wright's desk. *Coincidence,* he thought. Probably not, but he had no idea of the connection. Will made a mental note to do some research on this company when he got back to London.

What secret lay in the house? There must be something in the house. Will thought back to the original telephone call from Toby. What did he say? Will tried to recall the exact words.

'I want to show you something,' were Toby's words, not 'I want to tell you something.' So what did he want to show Will?

Were there any clues when he was in the house the last time? He went over in his mind the exact steps he took from the moment he entered the house until the police arrived. There was nothing that helped. Then he remembered, there was the gun cabinet key in the middle of the hall. Why was that there? Toby's killer had used their own gun and the cabinet was locked anyway. Will got up and walked out into the hall and over to the gun cabinet. He had left it unlocked, which on reflection was stupid, as the intruder, if they didn't have their own gun, could have taken one of these and used it against Will.

Will studied the cabinet from outside and then removed all the guns and felt around the cabinet in case there were any secret compartments. He removed the drawer under the cabinet which apart from the boxes of shells contained various items for cleaning the guns. Will peered into the aperture where the drawer had been and there appeared to be nothing hidden inside. Will turned over the drawer to make sure nothing was taped to the underneath. He felt along the top of the cabinet, just dust.

Will stepped back from the cabinet. He felt that there had to be something here. He peered at the front and then at the side. Strangely, the sides seemed to be deeper than the depth inside the cabinet as if there was something between the cabinet and the wall. Will tapped the back wall of the cabinet. It sounded hollow but there was no obvious entry point. He looked at the drawer aperture running his fingers around the sides, the top and the bottom and then he found a small round opening in which there was a button. Will pressed it and the cabinet juddered open a few millimetres. The whole cabinet was on hinges and revealed a thin compartment the length of the cabinet with several shelves. On the top shelf was a stack of £50 pound notes, the second held an envelope and the bottom shelf housed a small automatic pistol. He took the envelope, it was unsealed and he slid out a sheet of paper. The only writing on the page was a list of five lines of eight numbers. It meant nothing to Will, but it was obviously important enough to keep concealed, so he put the sheet back in the envelope and slipped it into his jacket pocket. Will left the money but for some reason that he could not explain, he also pocketed the pistol.

Will closed the cabinet, replaced the drawer, all the guns and locked it up. He placed the key back on the shelf where he had put it on his last visit. He looked around and satisfied everything looked the same as he had found it, he decided there was nothing more to be found in the house and that it was time to leave before it got dark.

With a certain amount of anxiety, Will opened the front door and stepped outside towards his car. He half-waited for the sound of a gunshot but there was none. He replaced the key under the plant pot, got into the car, started the engine and headed out of the drive. The sun was going down and Will knew it would be dark in a few minutes and decided that he would stay the night, again in the Ballachulish Hotel.

It was the same receptionist behind the desk from Will's last visit.

'Good afternoon, sir, nice to see yee again.'

'Yes, good afternoon. Could I have a room please?' asked Will.

'Would yee like the same room you had last time? I believe it is free,' said the receptionist tapping into a keyboard and looking at a screen that was on the desk.

'Yes, please,' replied Will.

The receptionist titled his head to one side with a slight smirk on his face as if he knew the answer before he asked the question.

'Would yee like a toothbrush again, too, sir?'

'Yes, please, and thank you.'

'I will have one sent up, sir. How long will yee be staying?'

'Hopefully, just one night, provided the snow doesn't cause any difficulties tomorrow.'

'The forecast is for a better day tomorrow,' ventured the receptionist. 'Just to remind you, sir, dinner is from 7 p.m. and breakfast from 7 a.m.'

Will thanked him and moved into the bar. Once again the receptionist scuttled through a passage and appeared behind the bar.

'Large whisky, please,' requested Will.

'Same as last time, sir?' the receptionist asked.

'That will be fine, thank you.' It struck Will strange that the receptionist remembered so well what he had drunk previously. Perhaps clientele was light in this part of the Scotland.

Will took his drink and sat by the window looking out over the eastern edge of the Loch.

There was something that was rumbling around the back of Will's mind that he thought was important to his situation but he couldn't quite find it.

He went over in his mind everything that had happened to him since he had discovered Toby's body. None of it really made any sense.

Why had Toby called him?

Was it the sheet of paper that was hidden in the gun cabinet? Was it this paper that Toby was going to show him? If so, what does it mean?

Who were the two men who responded to Will's 999 call? There weren't policemen!

What about Java PLC, what is the connection there?

Why had he been almost killed three times? Who was behind this and why him?

Out of all this, the only bright aspect was Jay. He thought he was probably in love with her. He ordered another drink and sat down again and thought he would give Jay a call to tell her what had happened. It was then that lightning struck in his mind and found what he was trying to grasp. It filled him with horror as he struggled with the likelihood of his thoughts and the ramifications.

Chapter Nineteen

Jay lived in a now gentrified area of Shoreditch in East London. The Town Hall was a venue for corporate events and next door was a very up-market restaurant.

Will turned into a road of terraced houses and found the house he was looking for. It was sandwiched between two fairly run down houses. The one on the left had a range of various motorbike parts in the front garden and the one on the right was piled high with old furniture. Jay's house had a tidy approach with a couple of terracotta pots filed with geraniums and other late flowering annual plants.

Will rang the bell.

Jay open the door dressed in a loose shirt and jeans.

'Will,' she said with surprise in her voice, 'come in.'

'I won't be stopping. I just wanted to confront you with something.'

'OK,' responded Jay questioningly.

'I have been thinking long and hard about what has happened to me over the last few weeks. Although I am far from answering most of the questions, there was only one person who knew I was traveling to Scotland, where I was nearly killed again. I don't know who you are working for and it really hurts me to say this but I am not going to see you again.'

With that Will turned and headed down the path.

'Wait. Will, I never told anyone,' called out Jay. But Will was already on the way to his car. He drove off and stopped around the corner and just sat there and cried. He had really thought he had found someone that he cared for. He wiped his face and thought, *You are on your own now, Will, so stop feeling sorry for yourself and get on and sort this out.*

As soon as Will arrived home, he phoned his office.

'Maria, it's Will Slater. Can you do me a favour please?'

'Of course, Mr Slater, what is it?' came the reply.

'I need you to do a search on a company called Java PLC. Last set of accounts and annual return, please.'

'Of course. Shall I e-mail the documents through to you?'

'Yes, please. When do you think you will be able to do it?'

'I will do it immediately. Should only take a few minutes.'

'Thanks, Maria. One more thing. Do we have a client number and a partner allocation?'

'Let me check,' there was a pause and then, 'Yes, there is a number and it is allocated to Sam.'

'Thanks again, Maria.'

'Pleasure, Mr Slater. Look forward to seeing you back here soon.'

'I hope so. Bye.' Will put down his phone.

Will opened up his inbox and waited for the documents to arrive.

Maria was as good as her word and within 10 minutes Will's inbox pinged with the new e-mail.

He first looked at the annual return and noted that the company was owned by an offshore trust in the British Virgin Islands. This didn't surprise him much as he had a feeling that the company was important to this whole scenario and that it was likely that the shareholders would not want to be easily recognised or contacted. Although the company was designated as a PLC – public liability company – it was not listed on any stock exchange and is what is called a vanity PLC. With a share capital of at least £50,000 it was able to use the letters "PLC". This was often used by people to make a company appear bigger or more credible than it actually was.

He then started to read through the accounts. The first page was the Directors Report which listed all the directors of the company. There was only one director.

Will sat transfixed for a few moments as he read the name.

"Mr William Slater."

Will sat back in his chair and let out a deep breath. How could this be? He knew nothing about the company. He flicked forward the pages of accounts on the screen and there was his signature at the foot of the balance sheet. Will peered at the signature on the page. It looked like his signature but it was forged. He then flicked back to the profit and loss account page.

Java PLC was a very profitable company. In the last year it had turnover of in excess of £20 million. Its costs and expenses were £15million so it had made £5million pounds profit before tax. It had a bank balance of £25 million and a similar level of reserves. So it had been trading at this level for a number of years.

He looked at the name of the company's auditors, Charles Foundler of Foundler & Co. with an office address in Brixton, South London. This would be Will's first port of call in the morning to find out more about Java PLC.

Chapter Twenty

Foundler & Co's offices were in an old office block in a side street just off the main high road in Brixton, South London. There was a board outside saying that there were offices for let. Probably not surprising as the offices looked run down, although there was a security guard sitting behind a reception desk in the lobby.

'Foundler & Co?' asked Will.

'Third floor man,' replied the security guard, barely looking up from the paper he was reading.

Foundler & Co was in a two-office suite. The main office, which housed the reception and general office and a smaller adjacent office.

Will knocked and walked through the frosted half-glassed door.

There were two people in the office. A man who looked to be in his fifties and was probably some type of accounts clerk and a woman in her twenties.

'Can I 'elp you?' The woman asked in a cockney voice.

'I would like to see Mr Foundler, please?'

'Ave you got an appointment?'

'No, but I should only be a few moments,' replied Will.

'Are you a client?' the cockney girl asked.

'Well, yes and no.'

The cockney girl titled her head to one side and gave Will a look that said 'surely you know'.

'What's yur name then?'

'Slater, William Slater.'

'I will check if 'e's in.'

The cockney girl knocked on the door to the other office and went in closing it behind her. Seconds later she reappeared.

'Mr Foundler will see yur,' and she stood holding open the door to his office.

'Thank you,' replied Will and walked into the second office.

Will judged that Foundler was a man in his sixties, he was short and quite fat and was wearing a three-piece suit that looked as if it was 40 years old. In fact everything in the office looked as if it was at least 40 years old.

Foundling stood but there was very little noticeable difference in height to when he had been seated. He had a quizzical look on his face.

'Sorry, my girl said you were William Slater. She must have misunderstood.'

'No, that is correct. Will Slater of Java PLC,' replied Will.

'No, there must be some mistake you are not Mr Slater of Java. I know him and it is definitely not you.'

'Ah, but that is the problem, Mr Foundling, I am Will Slater, the person who you met must have been impersonating me. I know nothing about Java and its activities, although I somehow seem to be the sole director. I wondered if I could ask you a few questions about the company as you are its auditors.'

'I am sorry Mr Slater or whatever your name is, all that information is confidential and I must ask you to leave immediately.'

'This is ridiculous, I am Will Slater, it is my address and details filed at Companies House as the Director of Java,' shouted Will.

'Shouting will get you nowhere. I don't care what you say, you are not the Will Slater that I communicate with and if you don't leave now I will call the police,' shouted back Foundler.

With that Will turned and strode out of the office leaving both doors wide open in some sort of protest as to his treatment.

As soon as Will had left the office, Foundler got up and closed his door and then picked up his phone and made a call.

Chapter Twenty-One

Will had to get back into Foundler's office and look through the Java file. Fortunately, it didn't look like the type of practice where the files were computerised so he hoped there would be plenty of hard copy documents that he could find. He hadn't worked out yet how he might be able to get into Foundling's office, although it seemed inevitable that it would involve a little breaking and entering, which would not do his professional status any good if he got caught. But at the moment, it would be lucky if he survived long enough to ever practice again.

As he walked down the stairs to reception, he thought he would reconnoitre the building for his next visit, which he imagined would be out of office hours. He stopped off on the second floor and walked to the end of the corridor. Most of the offices seemed occupied and at the end there was a fire exit. Simple push bar, no alarm and straight out onto the fire escape which led down to the street below. He noted the name on one of the office doors – Zenith Cleaning Services.

Will walked down the remaining two flights and stopped at reception to gather some more information.

'I notice there are some premises available for rent in the building,' Will said addressing the security guard.

'Yes, man on the 5th floor,' replied the guard.

'I can contact the agent from the details on the board outside but was interested in the security arrangements? Is there security here during all working hours?'

'Yea, man,' came the reply.

'Long day for you then,' stated Will.

'No, man we do two shifts. I do 8 a.m. to 2 p.m. and then another guard does until 8 at night.'

'What happens if I want to work outside those hours?' asked Will.

'You'll get a key. There's one or two who like to use the offices out of hours if you know what I mean?' said the guard winking at Will and tapping the side of his nose with his finger.

Will thought for a moment, not really sure what was meant but said, 'What, local ladies?'

'Wouldn't call them women, ladies, but you got the track man,' replied the guard.

Will thanked the security guard and headed back to his car.

Will reckoned he had to act quickly as he had put Foundler on his guard and he didn't want him destroying any information. However, he put Foundler down as a lazy man and thought whatever he was advised to do, he would take his time to act.

Will parked in a neighbouring road and walked around to the back of the block that housed Foundler's office to see where the fire escape emerged. He noticed a couple of CCTV cameras on several buildings and a pub around the corner from the building but out of sight of the fire escape.

Will headed home and decided on a plan of action. It was not without fault and had a number of unknowns but it was worth a try.

The following morning Will headed for a number of shops to buy his purchases for the afternoon and evening events.

After his shopping trip, Will assembled his purchases on the bed in the spare bedroom in his house. He then packed into a rucksack a bottle of water, four nutrition bars, a balaclava, the sort climbers wear in cold climates, a cloth cap, a pair of spectacles with clear glass, an anorak, a powerful torch, a newspaper and a book. He had also bought a long raincoat which reached his mid-calf and a leather hat with a very wide brim.

He drove his car and parked in a street about two roads away from the Brixton office block. With his rucksack, he entered the café across the road from the office and ordered a coffee. He looked at his watch 1.15. At 1.40 Will put on his clear glasses and walked across the road and into the office. It was the same guard as yesterday and as yesterday was busy reading the racing page of a newspaper and barely looked up as

Will said, 'Zenith, second floor,' and strode past the guard to the stairs. The guard grunted something but didn't bother to look up.

Will had timed his entrance just before the changeover of guards so the later shift would not noticed that he had not left the building. Will made his way up to the 4th floor gents' lavatory, entered a cubicle and locked the door and prepared for a 6-hour wait. He heard a few people enter the lavatory but imagined that most of the employees on this floor must be women as trade was very slow. Will read his book, drank some water and eat his nutrition bars.

By 7 p.m. there appeared to be no movement anywhere and he expected the security guard would just check all the lavatories before he locked up at 8 o'clock. Human nature told him that he would probably check the ladies lavatory less thoroughly than the gents. The lavatories were arranged with a different sex on each floor. Will went up to the 5th floor where there were empty offices and possibly less women employees. He opened the ladies lavatory door. He peered around and not surprising there was no one there. All the office had their light off so he suspected there would be no more use of the lavatory now. He decided to wait in the first cubicle, closest to the door. He didn't shut the door but managed to wedge it open, with a wodge of toilet paper, enough for it to look unoccupied but with no clear view of the toilet bowl on which he was going to stand when the guard did his round. The toilets didn't have seat covers so Will was going to have to balance on the seat itself. After a few practices he found it was better to rest his feet on the porcelain bowl with the seat up, sit on the cistern with his rucksack clutched to his chest. He suspected that the guard would start at the top and work down. He would probably also commence his tour so he had finished it by 8 o'clock. Sure enough, at about 7.45 Will heard someone walking up the stairs and positioned himself with his feet off the floor. The lavatory door was pushed open and a voice called out, 'Anyone in here?'

Will thought that the guard would switch off the light and move downstairs. But he didn't, he heard the guard come into the lavatory and make his way down the cubicles and then entered one. Will heard him down load in a cacophony of splashes and farts. There was quiet for a moment. Then the rasping of cheap, course toilet paper, a quick splash under the tap, light off and door closed.

Will waited a few moments and climbed down from his perch and sat on the toilet rim. He looked at his watch − 19.55. Will waited until 20.15 and he left the cubicle and opened the door to the lavatory. He peered down the corridor towards the stairs and seeing it clear, stepped out.

As he did so, from the other direction, a huge black hand grabbed him by the throat and pinned him to the wall.

'Yuz, think I am some kinda fool and didn't know yuz in that toilet! What you doing here man robbin uz?'

Will could hardly breathe and was trying to pull the security guard's huge arm from his neck.

'Can't breathe, can't breathe,' rasped Will.

The guard slackened his hold.

'Am meeting someone,' Will said.

'Who man?'

Will thought quickly.

'The Cockney girl at the accountants,' replied Will.

With that, the guard slackened his grip and smiled.

'Should 'ave told me man and saved this agro. How much she chargin' you man? I had 'er a few weeks back meself.'

Will had no idea what the going rate for a shag with a prostitute was. He didn't want to say too much but didn't want it to sound ridiculously low either.

'One hundred and twenty five pounds,' said Will and waited for the reaction.

With that the guard let go of Will's neck and bent down laughing pumping his hand against his thighs.

'Yuz, been done man. Must've seen you coming with all your lardy da.' The guard could hardly talk through his deep belly laughter.

'I did 'er for fifty last week,' and burst into more gales of laughter.

The guard suddenly stopped and placed his hand at Will's neck again.

'Still yuz brakin' and enterin', I could call the pigs man.'

'Am sure we can come to some arrangement. What about a hundred pounds?'

'Umm,' replied the guard.

'OK, two hundred that's all I have got.'

The guard let go of Will's neck and burst into laughter again.

'That's another four shags with that tart. Tell you what, man, for that I will let you into their office to wait your enjoyment.'

They both walked down two flights of stairs, the guard open Foundler's offices and let Will in.

'Have a good time, it won't last long man, she doesn't do any extras, straight in and out,' and with that he left and Will could hear him laughing all the way down the stairs.

Although he had hoped not to have been seen, it was stroke of luck that he was in the offices without having to force any locks.

Chapter Twenty-Two

Will opened the door to Foundling's own office. He decided not to switch on the desk lamp but use his torch. Everywhere was very quiet, he left the main office door open and thought he would be able to hear anyone approaching up the stairs.

He went to the main filing cabinet in Foundling's room and opened the dividers up at "J". Sure enough there was a thick file of papers entitled "Java PLC – audit 31 December year end".

The file was divided up into sections. The first sections covered the balance sheet items, assets and liabilities and were sub-divided into fixed assets, debtors, bank balances and creditors. The second part of the file dealt with the trading activities and were made up of sections covering sales, purchases and expenses.

Will looked at the sections dealing with the assets first. There were no fixed assets as far as Will could tell, this was a virtual company, with no premises, just made up of financial transactions. This type of company is very difficult to trace. There were very few debtors – amounts owed to the company – so Will turned to the "bank" section. The company had £25 million in cash and it appeared that it was spread over five bank accounts all in the British Virgin Islands in one bank. There was a neat hand written schedule of the account numbers and address of the bank. Will took a photograph of this schedule with his phone. He then moved onto the creditor section – amounts owed by the company. There was a large amount of £2 million owing to a company with an Eastern European sounding name, a few thousand owed to the auditors for their year-end work and an amount owed to HMRC for tax.

The profit and loss sections were far more interesting. There was a long list of all the sales invoices with company names and a list of purchases but with relatively few names. The expenses were minimal. Will took copies of various pages on his phone. He replaced to file back into the cabinet and flicked through the files to see if there was one with his personal name. As he was doing so another name caught his eye. Will didn't think much of it as it was a common name. He then spotted the file with his name and was about to open it when he heard voices and laughter from the stairwell. He put the file in his rucksack and closed the outer office door and retreated into Foundling's office switching off his torch. The voices got nearer. There was a man and a woman and he recognised the woman's voice as belonging to the Cockney receptionist.

'Leave me 'lone till we get inside,' the woman said.

They had reached the outer office door.

'Cor fuck me I forgot to lock up when I left earlier,' she said.

'I thought that was the general idea, at least, that is what I paid my money for.' Will heard the man say.

'What – ha very funny,' replied the woman.

'Let's do it in the old geezer's room,' said the man.

'Not bloody likely, not getting all yur cum on 'is leather desk. Mine will wipe down after,' replied the Cockney.

Will waited a couple of minutes until he heard some heavy breathing and grunts, he put on his balaclava and pulled it down over his face, put on his wide brimmed hat and walked out into the main office. The Cockney was lying on a desk and had her legs wrapped around her customer's neck, while he was co-joined to the Cockney at his waist with his trousers and pants around his ankles.

'Have a lovely evening,' called out Will as he open the main office door and headed for the stairs.

'Fucking hell, who was that?' shouted the Cockney. 'Get after that peeping bastard.'

Will swept down the stairs to the floor below and sprinted down the hallway and out through the fire exit. He ran down the fire escape into the street below and around the corner, removing his balaclava as he went. He immediately slowed down to a brisk walk with his head down as he knew he was now within sight of a CCTV camera. He stepped into the door of the nearby pub taking off his hat and slipping on his glasses as he stepped through the door.

The pub was reasonably busy but there was no one standing at the bar.

Will stepped up and ordered a pint of Guinness.

'Where is the gents?' Will asked the barman.

'Just around the corner mate.'

Will put a ten-pound note on the bar.

'Thanks, will pick up the change when I get back,' replied Will.

Will entered the gents' lavatory where he changed his long coat and wide brimmed hat for an anorak and a flat cap. Stuffing the disrobed items into his rucksack.

He returned to the bar, picked up his change and pint and sat at a table just behind the door he had entered through. He pushed his rucksack out of sight, had a long draught of his beer and picked up the paper he had also put in his rucksack earlier and waited.

Within two minutes, the door crashed open and the cockney's customer stood at the entrance with a furious look on his face scouring the people in the pub. He walked over to the bar and asked the barman whether anyone in a long coat and hat had just run in.

'What's it to you, mate?' replied the barman.

'Never you mind' was the response.

Will didn't look up and continued reading his paper but from the corner of his eye he could see the man walking around the pub looking at the customers. When he was satisfied no one looked like the office intruder, he left the pub.

Will waited another 10 minutes, finished his Guinness and left the pub via the other door. He walked to his car which was in an adjacent street and drove home.

When Will got home, he printed out the photocopied pages that he had taken on his phone, poured himself a large whisky and sat down at the dining room table. He spread out the copies and took out the correspondence file he had taken from the office.

He looked at the copied pages. First he looked at the schedule of sales invoices. The names of the companies meant nothing to him. Will searched the names on the internet but nothing came up. This led Will to believe that these were either not real companies or needed to be under the "radar". Then Will looked at the schedule of purchases. There only seemed to be one company that Java purchased from, the Eastern European sounding name, Sljonic Inc. Will looked up this name on the Internet too. This time he got a hit. The web site told Will that Sljonic dealt in all types of industrial hardware, both new, second hand and salvaged, ranging from cranes and bulldozers to drills and angle grinders. None of this made any sense to Will. He couldn't understand how anyone could make such huge profits on second-hand merchandise. The only clue was that the company advertised itself as finding any hardware product that a customer required. Will decided to call the company the following morning.

Will then opened up the correspondence file. There was little in the file. Will imagined most of the communication would be done via e-mail. However, to meet anti-money laundering regulations there would be a copy of a utility bill and a certified picture identity from a driving license or passport for the only director of the company, which was Will.

The utility bill was one of Will's, no surprise there, but the driving license was a forgery as the picture purporting to be Will was not his picture.

Will sat staring at the picture on the driving license. The face that stared back from the fake was Sam Brewer, one of Will's partners. He couldn't believe it. Sam, but why him? Will looked at his watch, 11.30 p.m. It was late but he decided to phone one of his other partners, George Wright.

'George, it's Will, I am sorry it is late but I need to speak to you about Sam. He seems to have impersonated me in some sort of scheme which I think may be illegal.'

'I can't believe that Will. Why would he want to do that? Have you got any evidence?' asked George.

'Yes, plenty. Can we meet tomorrow so I can show you?'

They agreed to meet the following evening at the Grenadier at 6.30 p.m.

Chapter Twenty-Three

The following morning, Will phoned Sljonic Inc.

A male voice answered, 'Sljonic.'

'Good morning, my name is Mike Wall.' Will decided not to use his real name. 'I work for the accountants who prepare the accounts for a company called Java PLC and have a few questions in regard to the outstanding amounts owing from Java to your company. We have been passed all the paperwork to prepare the accounts but we don't seem to have any invoices to substantiate the amount owing to your company. Who am I speaking to please?'

'My name is Josef Mellnic. I am not sure I can help you. I will need to speak to my boss. Hold a moment please.'

Will waited on the line while he imagined the boss was asked the question.

Mellnic came back on the line again.

'I am sorry, Mr...?'

'Wall,' replied Will.

'I am sorry, Mr Wall, my boss says that he needs permission from the company to let you have details of the transactions. He suggests you contact them and ask for the information. My boss also says when you speak to them tell them they owe us a lot of money and we need payment immediately or there will be a problem. OK?'

'I suppose so but I would have liked the information,' replied Will.

'Don't forget to tell them about the money.' Then the line went dead.

Will sat and pondered. *A dead end there*, he thought. He hoped he would get further when he met George a little later.

The Grenadier public house, situated at Hyde Park Corner in the mews just behind the Lanesborough Hotel, was originally built in 1720 as the Officers Mess for The First Royal Regiment of Foot Guards. The Regiment became famous by being the only regiment in the British Army to be named for one of its battle honours as a result of the heroism that it showed whilst fighting off the French Grenadiers at Waterloo in 1815.

The Grenadier became a licensed premise in 1818 to serve as The Guardsman Public House. The Grenadier was famously known as the Duke of Wellington's Officers Mess and was even frequented by King George IV.

The name change to "The Grenadier" is reputed to have been after a young Grenadier, affectionately named Cedric by locals, whom is said to have been caught cheating at a game of cards. The story goes that his comrades savagely beat him to death as a punishment. An exact date as to when this happened is unknown, but it is presumed that that fateful night was in the month of September, as this is the time of year that The Grenadier receives an onslaught of supernatural and spooky activity! Past visitors of the pub have attempted to pay off Cedric's debt by attaching money to the ceiling, which, after over a century, has been totally covered with transatlantic money.

George was seated at a table just inside the door, nursing a glass of red wine. He looked up as Will walked in.

'What would you like?' asked George.

Will looked down at George's glass.

'I will have one of those, too, please,' replied Will.

When George sat down again with Will's drink, Will removed various papers from his briefcase. One by one, he showed them to George explaining the significance of each and filing in the background.

'Wow,' said George, 'I would never have believed it if you hadn't shown me. However, I still don't understand why. Have you shown this to Sara?'

'No, I thought I would show you first and see what you think.'

'I think we need to confront him with this and see what he has to say,' said George.

'Yes, I agree. Can we do this tomorrow morning in the office?' suggested Will.

'OK, let's do it,' replied George. 'Another drink?'

'No, thanks, let's go, I don't feel like drinking anymore,' said Will.

'Yep, OK. Which way are you going?' asked George.

'Piccadilly line to Earls Court and then the Wimbledon line and you?'

'I will walk as it is not far to Knightsbridge,' replied George.

Both men left the pub and said their goodbyes, Will reminding George that they were going to approach Sam first thing in the morning and then he walked down to Hyde Park Corner tube station.

The station was very busy and he could not get on the first train that came through. By the time the next one was approaching, he was standing near to the edge of the platform. Will felt a hard nudge in the back and suddenly found himself falling forward in front of the incoming train.

Will called out 'Help!' as he fell forward off the platform towards the rails when a large hand grabbed his coat collar and yanked him back onto the platform. As Will regained his balance, he turned to see an enormous man still holding onto his collar.

'Man, you were almost a goner there,' he said.

'Ahhh, thank you so much,' said Will in a very shaky voice. 'I was pushed. Did you see who pushed me?'

'All I saw mate, was a bloke with red hair standing behind you. I turned to look at the train and the next thing I saw was you tumbling forward. Cor, you didn't half give me a fright. I thought you was a goner,' the man said repeating himself. 'You'll need to report this to the police.'

'Perhaps it was an accident,' said Will.

'I don't know about that mate but it has quite turned me over,' said the man. 'I need to get home.'

The train that would have caused Will's death had departed and the next one was thundering into the platform.

'I am getting this one,' said the man.

'Well, thank you again for saving my life. I feel I owe you something.'

'Naw, my good deed for the day,' and the man gave Will a half-smile and got into the train.

Will didn't feel like travelling on the tube anymore that day so made his way back to street level and hailed a black cab to take him home.

When Will got home, he felt pretty awful. He thought it must be the shock from almost dying. He poured himself a very large whisky and sat down at the kitchen table to try and assimilate what had just happened to him. Could it have been an accident? There were a lot of people on the station but the nudge was very hard and if it had been an accident why was the red haired man still not on the platform. He couldn't have got into the train as it was not in the station by the time he had been rescued by the stranger. Surely, he would have been still standing behind Will. It must have been deliberate which sent more horrific thoughts surging through Will's mind. He poured himself another drink to try and calm his nerves. *OK*, Will thought, *it has all to do with Toby's death, Java and Sam Brewer impersonating me. That is what I have to sort out*. Will thought about phoning Dawkin and telling him that he had almost been killed but didn't expect to get much sympathy from that quarter so thought he would call him after he had had a face to face with Sam the following day. At least, he would have George to corroborate his story.

Will looked at his watch – 8 p.m. It was late but he suspected someone would still be in the office.

'Slater & Craig,' the voice answered from the other end of the phone.

Will recognised the voice as one of the legal assistants.

'Rachael, it's Will Slater, how are you?' asked Will.

'Good, thank you, Will, and you?'

'Not too bad. Could you do me a favour and see if Sam is in the office first thing in the morning as I would like to pop over to see him for a few minutes?' asked Will.

'Let me have a look at his electronic diary.'

There was a pause before Rachel replied.

'He seems to be working from home all day tomorrow, Will.'

'OK, thanks Rachel,' and Will put down the phone.

So a trip to the country tomorrow morning! thought Will. In some respects perhaps the discussion that was going to take place would be best out of the office in any case.

Will decided he would not warn Sam that he was coming but just pitch up to keep him off his guard.

Chapter Twenty-Four

The cockney girl opened the door to the main office and noticed it was unlocked and that the light was on in her boss's office.

The old man is in early this morning, the cockney thought as she busied herself making coffee for them both. When it was ready, she knocked on his door, opened it and for a moment was not sure what she was seeing, but then she realised and dropped the mug of coffee on the floor and screamed at the same time. Foundler sat at his desk, looking towards the door with a surprised expression on his face and with a small neat hole in his forehead just above the eyes and a trickle of blood down the side of his nose.

Sergeant Edgar walked into Dawkin's office.

'We have a murder Gov, in Brixton. An accountant, discovered by his secretary when she got to work this morning.'

'OK,' said Dawkin as he picked up his jacket, 'let's take a look. SOCO been informed?'

'Yes, sir. I understand they are already on site.'

When they got to Foundling's office, Dawkin and Edgar put on gloves and placed blue covers over their shoes. In the corner of the main office, the cockney girl was being comforted by a woman PC.

A man in white overalls and a facemask was hunched over the victim.

'What have we got Groome?' Dawkins asked of the medical examiner.

'Dead about 12 hours, so some time last evening. Single bullet wound to the head, immediate death. Looks quite professional to me,' said the examiner.

'Think you should leave the suppositions to us if you don't mind, you stick with the facts,' replied Dawkin.

'Point taken, Inspector, wouldn't wish to tread on your toes. Think we have finished here. As soon as you say we will get the body back where I can examine it in more detail.'

'OK, fine,' said Dawkin.

Dawkin turned to the Edgar, 'What did the girl have to say?'

'Nothing, really, just that he was in his office when she got in. She did say that they had had a break in a couple of nights ago although as far as they can tell nothing was taken.'

'Did they report it?' asked Dawkin.

'No, as apparently the girl was entertaining a "friend" in the office when they disturbed the intruder. He ran off down the fire escape and her "friend" chased after but lost him.'

'Umm, maybe a coincidence, although I doubt it. I noticed that they have a security bloke at reception. Have a chat with him and find out if anyone was on duty at the time and might have seen something. See if there are any CCTV cameras around about, we might be able to pick up who killed him and who broke in earlier.'

'Right you are Gov, on the case,' replied Edgar.

Chapter Twenty-Five

At the same time as Foundling's body was being discovered, Will was driving to Sam Brewer's house which was in a small village outside of Petersfield in East Sussex. George had phoned first thing in the morning to say that he couldn't leave the office as he had an important client to meet. Will agreed that he would go alone and let George know what happened after the meeting.

Will stopped his car across from the gate to Sam's house.

The house had a circular drive that led up to a very spectacular house. Will had not been here before but even on Sam's large profit share from the partnership, he wondered how he could afford a property of this size. He pulled across the road and opened the car window and pressed a buzzer by the gate.

'Yes,' came the voice from the intercom. Will recognised it as Sam's.

'Sam, it's Will, can I come in please?'

'What! Well, yes, I suppose so, why?'

'Think it would be better if we did this inside,' replied Will.

'OK.'

The gates started to open and Will drove up to the house.

The house and gardens were even more impressive from inside the gate. The gardens had all been designed and were immaculate and apart from the house itself there was a large garage, some outbuilding and what looked like stables towards the rear of the house.

As Will got out of his car, the front door opened and Sam emerged onto the front step.

'What are you doing here, Will? I thought we all agreed that you would leave us alone until Toby's murder had been cleared up. Anyway, it is not very convenient as I am in the middle of something.' Sam seemed to be quite agitated.

'We need to talk about Java. I have found out everything.'

'I don't know what you are talking about so please leave now.' Sam pointed to the gate at the end of the drive.

'Sam, this has gone too far, I have nearly been murdered four times, the last time was last night when someone tried to push me in front of a tube train.'

Sam seemed to metaphorically slump.

'My god, that is awful.' He looked down at the ground and said, 'You had better come in.'

Sam led Will into the expensively furnished lounge.

'It is my name on all the company documents but it is your picture on the anti-money laundering documentation. I guess it is you who Foundling thought was me,' stated Will.

'I know nothing about any of that Will. I was not involved in the set up. I was told that my details were needed and for that I would get a handsome payment. I needed the money for this place,' said Sam waving his hands around indicating all of the house, 'it costs a fortune.'

Will was silent hoping that Sam would continue talking, which he did.

'I thought that was all I would have to do but then I was asked to send emails and effectively become the face of Java to the outside world. I would have told you but I was being paid huge sums of money for very little.'

'You must have known whatever you were doing must have been illegal?' said Will.

'Yes, at first, I thought about it very often and I know it sounds strange but I didn't know what to tell anyone. I had no names and all the transactions were being authorised by me. I didn't even know what was actually going on. I spoke to Foundling but all he said was that his job was to enter the transactions in the books and produce the accounts. Money was paid into my bank account on a regular basis and I began to rely on the money for my life style, so after a year or so and as no one had asked any questions I just went on with it.'

'But that is impossible, you must have had contact with someone in the first place, you must know his name?'

Sam was just about to say something when there was huge bang from the hall and it sounded as if the front door had been blown off.

Sam leapt up, followed by Will and both rushed out of the lounge.

Chapter Twenty-Six

Mellnic, was a wiry Eastern European, with course features, and drove the large Mercedes up to the gates of a large house in Sussex.

'Shall I ring the bell boss?'

'Naw, Josef, use the hammer,' was the reply.

Mellnic opened the boot and removed a long cylindrical metal barrel, which he then swung against the outside gate. The gate burst open with the first swing. Mellnic put the tool back in the boot and drove up to the front door.

Mellnic and the other three incumbents of the car got out and looked at the front door.

'What this time boss?' asked Mellnic.

'Same again, let's surprise him,' was the reply.

As Sam and Will rushed into the hall they saw the front door was wide open and standing in the gap were four very unsavoury men, one holding a cylindrical barrel with a handle that Will had seen the police use on television to break down doors.

'What the hell is going on,' shouted Sam, 'who the fuck are you?'

The one holding the door-opening implement stood aside and in walked one of the other men, flanked by two others.

'Ah, Mr Brewer and Mr...?' The man said looking in Will's direction.

'He is one of my partners and is just leaving. Off you go Will,' said Sam.

'I don't think anyone will be leaving yet,' replied the man.

Will thought he had an eastern European accent, which fitted with the overall look of the man. The one who had spoken appeared to be the leader of the group. He was shorter than the other two and was dressed in an expensive looking dark blue overcoat, although it was not overly cold.

'Let's go into that room and discuss what we have come for Mr Brewer,' said the leader, pointing to the lounge whilst removing his leather gloves. The other two were much larger and both had lived in faces, with broken noses and scars. They spread out either side of their leader and drew pistols from their pockets.

They all walked into the lounge.

'Why don't you two sit down,' said the leader in a very menacing tone that was more of an order than a request.

Will could see that Sam was afraid and indeed Will was feeling rather nervous, too, but after the last few weeks nothing seemed to be impossible anymore.

'You owe us money, Mr Brewer, a lot of money and we want it now. Why have you not paid it into the agreed bank account? Or have you spent it all on this luxurious house?' The man waved his arms around looking at the room.

'No, of course not, I have the money I just need to transfer it,' replied Sam.

'Then why have you not done it yet? We have lost patience Mr Brewer.'

'I will. I will tomorrow,' exclaimed Sam.

'Not good enough, Mr Brewer, we want it now. How can we persuade you of this?'

The man looked across at Will.

'And you are?'

'Will Slater,' said Will.

'I seem to know that name,' the leader replied, 'Perhaps Mr Slater can help you, Mr Brewer.' The man snapped his fingers and one of his companions strode across the room and replaced his pistol with a nasty looking knife.

'Stand up, Mr Slater,' the leader said.

'No, I don't think I will, thank you,' replied Will.

'Stand up,' shouted the man.

Will reluctantly stood up where upon the companion with the knife grabbed Will by the neck and pushed the knife against his throat.

The leader turned to Sam.

'Now, Mr Brewer if you don't transfer the funds I regret to inform you that Mr Slater will die in a pool of blood on this exquisite and no doubt very expensive carpet. I am sure Mrs Brewer would be very upset by the mess.'

Will was now very frightened.

'Please, do it Sam,' exhorted Will.

'Yes, you heard the very good advice from your legal adviser, Mr Brewer.'

'I don't have the details of the bank accounts. They have been mislaid,' replied Sam.

'Mislaid, mislaid. We are not talking about your car keys. We are talking about millions of pounds,' shouted the leader.

'When I say mislaid, I mean the list has been stolen and we don't know where it is,' Sam screamed back.

'That is a pity for Mr Slater,' and the man nodded to his companion.

Will felt the pressure of the point of the knife against his neck.

'Drop your weapons,' came a voice from the open doorway.

Everyone turned and there stood Inspector Allan, or whatever was his real name, together with his red-haired sidekick, Brown, and several others pointing their guns. At that moment, all Will could see was the red hair of Brown and the image at the tube station.

'It was you who pushed me in the tube,' called out Will.

Brown's attention was drawn to Will for a second which allowed one of the Eastern European's men to fire at Brown with a devastating result and he crumpled to the ground. The gunman was immediately shot in a reply volley from one of Allan's men.

Will felt that he was in the middle of the 'OK, Corral' and was even more amazed when tucked in behind them all, also with a gun raised, was Jay.

The general confusion enabled Will to shove his captor to one side. Another shot rang out from one of the Eastern Europeans and the new entrants to the party dived for the floor. Will turned and saw that Sam had produced a gun from somewhere and looked as if he was about to fire when a red patch appeared in his chest and he fell to the floor. Will turned and saw Jay pointing her gun at him. He could see the finger squeeze on the trigger. Will dived to his left and felt a searing pain in his side and then nothing.

Chapter Twenty-Seven

After he had broken down the front door and his boss had entered the house, Mellnic stared at the house and imagined what it must be like to live here. He had been brought up in a tiny house in Serbia. As he suspected the meeting inside would take a few minutes, he decided to walk around the side of the house to look at the rear. As he was looking at the swimming pool, he heard a number of vehicles approaching the house at speed. He was alarmed and rushed to the corner of the house and saw three black cars pull up. The doors opened and a number of people including a woman, all armed, leapt out. About six ran towards the front door but two ran to the back of the house directly towards where Mellnic was standing. He turned and sprinted towards a small outhouse where pool furniture was stored. The door was partly open and he had just enough time to dive in before the men came around the corner of the building. He crouched down but the men were interested in the back door to the house and not the pool.

Mellnic then heard shooting from the house and the two men broke down the back door and rushed into the house. Mellnic waited a few moments but thought that it was time to try and get away. He moved carefully towards the front of the house. There was nobody there and Mellnic thought about taking the Mercedes and leaving but should his boss survive the shooting, which he doubted would happen, he would wonder why the car was not there and anyway, he would have been heard driving away. So keeping under the cover of the trees in the garden, Mellnic made his way to the broken down gate and out into the road. He heard more vehicles approaching so he hid behind a tree across the road from the house. He had a good, if distant, view of the front of the house and the drive. After a minute the vehicles he had heard approaching came into view.

Several police cars and two ambulances. While Mellnic watched from his cover some other vehicles arrived, this time two white vans and some ominous looking black vans which Mellnic assumed were undertaker's vehicles. He saw two people being taken to the ambulances, which rushed off with their sirens screaming. He then saw a handcuffed man being lead to one of the police cars, Mellnic was sure this was his boss. So he was still alive. Mellnic was not sure whether he was pleased or not. In any case, it would be a long while before he was free again. Mellnic ducked down as the police cars passed by him. He waited a while longer until three bodies were loaded into the back of the black vans. After they had passed by Mellnic's hiding place at a more sedate pace, he thought it was wise to move. He decided to walk in the opposite direction to all the traffic movement and prepared for a long walk but at least he was alive and uncaptured. It would give him plenty of time to make a plan of action.

Chapter Twenty-Eight

'Gov, we have had a look through all the CCTV footage around Foundling's office,' informed Sergeant Edgar to his boss.

'Well, anything?'

'Yes and no, Gov. We haven't got anything on the murder but we have got a man who we think was the intruder leaving the rear of the building a couple of days earlier. The girl described him as wearing a balaclava over his head. We pick him up on the CCTV around the corner, and can see him taking off the balaclava as he runs, presumably to avoid suspicion from anyone who sees him, but replaces the large hat and keeps his head down as if he knows where the cameras are. We see him enter the pub, taking off his large hat as he enters. A few minutes later a bloke who looks agitated enters the same pub. We think he is the girl's "friend" but he comes out of the other door a few minutes later presumably not having seen the intruder.'

'Did you continue watching to see when the intruder left?' asked Dawkin.

'Yes, Gov. There were a few comings and goings but no one dressed in a long coat and large hat left the pub until after closing.'

'So either the intruder lives in the pub, which I doubt, or he changed his appearance when he was inside,' said Dawkin as he scratched his chin. 'Get down to the pub and speak to the landlord and see if he remembers anything. If the intruder did know where the cameras were, he must have cased the area previously. Look back at the CCTV footage for, say, a week before the break in and see if anything comes up.'

'OK, Gov, on it,' replied Edgar.

Chapter Twenty-Nine

Mellnic made his way back to London. All his possessions and documents were in the house that he rented with, he assumed, his now two deceased friends, in Willesden, North London.

Mellnic was unsure whether the police would have the address yet. The boss was always strict that no one should have any details with them in case of the eventuality that had just occurred. He approached the corner of his road and stood looking casually around as if checking his location. There appeared to be no one unusual in the road so he walked past the house on the opposite side checking surreptitiously the cars on both sides of the road. There were all empty. He got to the end of the road and crossed over and walked back to his door. He walked up the path and rang the bell and turned around as if waiting for someone to come to the door. There still didn't appear to be anyone interested in him so he used his key to enter the house. He quickly packed all his possessions, picked up his passport and those of his compatriots, together with the small amount of cash in the house. He did one quick sweep of the house to make sure there was nothing to connect him and left the way he had come in and walked quickly to the nearest tube station.

Chapter Thirty

Everything appeared to be white. Will's brain drifted in and out of a spectrum of activity that ranged from no activity at all to a state where there was a vague recognition of some bodily life. During the more lucid periods of brain activity, the subconscious implied that Will might be lying down but there was no pain or sensations in his body at all. Time came and went and his brain engaged sometimes, other times, it didn't. Occasionally, his brain emitted a different sensation, some movement of his body or part of his body. This sensation became more regular and slowly his brain could sense parts of the body, first his arms and then his legs. His brain was still unable to get his limbs to work but it knew where they were in relation to it. Then his brain started hearing sounds, first noises and then voices. His brain tried to understand what was being said but that was beyond it at the moment. After a period of activity, his brain closed everything down for a while but each time it woke it seemed to recognise more of its close surroundings. Sounds became clearer and it began to recognise all parts of the body. His brain could now understand the voices and realised that mainly the voices were speaking about him. Will tried to speak but it was unable to do so.

Then, suddenly, he woke up.

Will opened his eyes and wished he hadn't. A searing pain flashed through his head and Will looked around. He heard a chair scrapping and a face appeared over the bed. The face disappeared and Will heard a door opening and a voice called out 'he's awake'. Will closed his eyes.

Will opened his eyes again and looked around. He was in a hospital room with various pieces of equipment attached to him.

The door opened and in came a man, who Will assumed was a doctor, together with a nurse.

'Good to see you awake again, Mr Slater, my name is Dr Lystern. How do you feel?'

'Groggy, feeling sick and a terrible pain in my head,' Will replied.

'We can sort that out,' the doctor said turning to the nurse.

Just then the door opened and in walked the man who had peered at Will and who apparently had been sitting at the end of Will's bed waiting for him to awaken. He wore a policeman's uniform and he looked expectantly at the doctor, the nurse and then Will.

'The authorities would like to ask Mr Slater some questions.'

'Impossible,' replied the doctor, 'not for some time. Please leave immediately.'

The policeman looked surprised but after a few seconds of shuffling his feet and murmuring under his breath, he complied.

'We will leave an officer outside the room until Mr Slater is fit to answer our questions,' he said as he left the room.

The doctor shrugged and instructed the nurse on the administration of more drugs.

'I will be back later, Mr Slater, to see how you are progressing,' and with that the doctor left too.

The nurse changed a drip bag that was attached via a tube to Will's wrist through a cannula.

'That should help you rest, Mr Slater,' the nurse said.

Will closed his eyes and drifted off to sleep.

When Will awoke again, he opened his eyes more slowly this time and gazed around the room, trying to remember why he was there. He had a vague memory of events leading up to his hospitalisation. He could recall that he was at Sam Brewer's house and then there was a shooting and then he remembered with a pang of regret that seemed to penetrate deep into Will's body that it was Jay who had shot him. Will closed his eyes and tears seeped through his closed lids. Will drifted off to sleep again.

Sometime later Dr Lystern returned and sat in a chair beside Will's bed.

'How long have I been here, Doctor?' asked Will.

'About five days, Mr Slater. You have had a nasty bash on the head that we were very concerned about.'

'I don't understand doctor, I thought I was shot, I saw the shooter and felt the pain.'

'You were, indeed, shot, but nothing compared to the bash on the head. A flesh wound by comparison, although it will be painful for a while. I, also, doubt you would have seen the person who shot you unless you have eyes in the back of your head, as you were shot from behind.'

'That's impossible I know who shot me.'

'Well,' replied the doctor, 'I have seen a lot of bullet wounds in my time and I can assure you the bullet entered from behind you and exited in the front. So the shooter could not have been standing in front of you.'

Will looked confused.

'And the head, how did that happen?' asked Will.

'It is a bit unclear, as I understand from the police and the medics who attended the scene, there were a lot of injuries and bodies; but the note on your admittance sheet stated that you had received a blow to the side of the head as well as a gunshot wound. I was told that you were found lying beside a low glass table which had your blood on it. So it appears that you somehow hit your head with great force against the corner of the table.'

'Oh, I see,' replied Will.

'How is your memory? You seem to have good recall.'

'I think it is fine, I can remember who I am, why I am here and the incidents leading up to it.'

'Good. Mr Slater, there is policeman who wants to see you and I think you are probably OK to see him for a short while. Is that OK with you?'

Will nodded.

'I will tell him only 10 minutes, until you are stronger.'

The doctor left the room.

A few minutes later the door open and the man known to Will as Inspector Allan stood in the doorway.

'You,' exclaimed Will, 'you aren't a policeman, it was one of your team who tried to kill me, he tried to push me in front of a tube train. I know it was him by his red hair,' said Will weakly. 'I saw him shot at the Sam's house,' added Will.

'I think I need to explain quite a lot. May I sit down?' asked Allan.

'I can't stop you while I am lying here.'

Allan pulled up a chair and sat by Will's bed.

'My name is Allan, Harry Allan, I am not a policeman, I am part of the security service specialising in anti-terrorism. I am from a department called SO 15 which is a specialist operations branch within the Met Police. We are part of the Counter Terrorism Command. Just to clear up matters, my colleague Brown, did not try to kill you. I don't know who tried to push you under a train but it was certainly not Brown. Fortunately, he was wearing a bullet proof vest, we all were when we entered Brewer's house, so he was just stunned by the bullets and am sure you will be pleased to know that apart from some bruising, he is fine.'

'Oh! OK,' said Will slightly apologetically.

We have been watching you for some time, Mr Slater.'

'What!' exclaimed Will. 'I am not a terrorist. Why have you been watching me?'

'Well, we believe that you have been set up as a front for funding the supply of arms to terrorists and military fractions, particularly, in the Middle East, but we need to know who is running the operation. This is operated, apparently, legitimately via a company called Java PLC, but I think you are already aware of this. The arms have been sourced from those left behind after the wars in the Balkans, Iraq, Afghanistan and various other skirmishes throughout the world. They have then been sold to terrorist organisations, including Isis. We believe a company called Sljonic Inc. is supplying the arms via Java but we don't know how they are getting them in the first place. The crowd that we had battle with at Brewer's house were from Sljonic. In fact, we believe we have the boss of Sljonic although he is not really talking at the moment. We believe that Java owed Sljonic a lot of money and they were trying to recover it from Brewer, their only contact with the company. A lot of money appears to have been made out of these deals but we aren't really interested in that, it is the fact that the arms are being sourced and financed out of the UK.

So we have been watching you to try and find out who is behind the company and the operation. Whoever it is, has very good connections and knowledge to be able to arrange the supply of the weapons, package them into saleable lots and then sell them to the terrorists,' explained Allan.

'But where do the terrorists get the money from to pay for the arms?' asked Will.

'Various places. Usually criminal,' replied Allan. 'Often they steal or rob banks. The larger more sophisticated military groups run drug and prostitution businesses. They, also, encourage their supporters to give them money. Sometimes even foreign states provide the funding. Either knowingly or not. So there is usually no shortage of funds to acquire the weapons. It is an economy in itself.'

Will was quiet as he took on board what Allan had told him and tried to make it relate to what he knew and what had happened to him.

'So if what you tell me is correct, why are you or someone else trying to kill me?' asked Will.

'I can assure you, Mr Slater, rather than trying to kill you, we have been trying to keep you alive. It has been difficult at times as you have not acted as we would have suspected an innocent person, and a lawyer, to act but we still believe in your innocent participation and it has probably helped us nail a few of the suspects along the way,' replied Allan.

'Well, do you know who is behind all this?' asked Will.

'Unfortunately, not entirely, we established that Sam Brewer was one of the main perpetrators and had impersonated you in connection with Java but we don't believe he was the main man. He didn't seem to have the connections and, quite frankly, the balls to deal with the type of people we are talking about. So we are still looking for him or them.'

'What about Toby McCloud, what was his involvement? He was not a criminal,' stated Will.

'We think he might have been coerced into funding the early transactions until it became self-financing. He had the banking connections and knew you very well. He may well have been blackmailed along the way. Anyway, we think that McCloud, had had enough, and was going to give you information which would have led us to the ringleader but he must have been suspected and they, whoever they are, decided to shut him up.'

'But how would they know that he was going see me let alone tell me anything?' asked Will.

'Well, they would have been tapping your phone, as I am afraid we must admit we are as well. That was how we had some idea of where you were going but, of course, so did the opposition.'

'Surely, there is some law about tapping people's phone. I mean, I know there is,' exclaimed Will.

'Normally, but where there is terrorism involved it is pretty easy to get permission. The opposition, however, must have had access to your home at some time to plant the bugs. Quiet easy. Knock on the door. Ask to read the meter or some other reason. Cleaner lets them in and "Bob's your uncle". Same with your mobile, leave it on your desk while you go to the loo and in seconds a device is attached. Brewer could have done it very easily.'

Will shook his head in disbelief.

'How long do you think I have been bugged?'

'Well, we have been tagging you for almost two years, not sure how long the oppo have.'

'I don't really socialise with members of the office at home but I did have them and all the partners over to a barbeque last summer to celebrate finalising a very difficult acquisition. Brewer could have done it then,' Will said with a quizzical look.

'Possibly, Brewer or anyone at your office,' replied Allan.

Will frowned at the thought of anyone else being involved.

'One thing we didn't understand was that Companies House write to company directors from time to time and we would have thought that you would have become aware of Java?' asked Allan.

'Yes, that is true but we often set up companies for clients and temporarily become directors until the management take over. Because of that we have staff members who deal with all the relevant forms and rarely do letters come to the partners. Companies House will write to the company secretary on occasions but we use a corporate vehicle for those services so all letters would be addressed to it. Only if the company is behind in its filing, will Companies House write to the Director at his home address. I assume that Sam made sure that this never occurred. When I phoned the office to obtain information on Java, I was told that the client was allocated to Sam. So all letters into the office would have gone to him first.'

'OK. Tell me did you find anything at McCloud's house? We searched it twice and found nothing,' asked Allan.

Will thought for the moment and remembered the piece of paper that he had found in the gun cabinet.

'No, nothing that I can recall but my memory is still hazy,' Will thought that the paper was important but he was still not sure about Allan, so he decided not to mention it.

The door opened and the doctor came in.

'I think Mr Slater should rest now.'

'OK, I think we have finished. I have arranged for a policeman to remain outside just in case of any uninvited visitors. Should you remember anything, please tell the officer outside to contact me. I hope we can find who is behind this as the authorities are keen to pin this all onto someone. Thank you, Mr Slater, we will speak again,' said Allan in a tone that left little doubt.

Both Allan and the doctor left the room. Will lay back in bed and closed his eyes but he didn't sleep as he went over everything that he had been told. What did Allan mean "pin this all on someone"? He also thought about Jay. He was pleased that she hadn't shot him but now that he knew she was part of the security services he realised that their relationship, if that was what it could be called, was a sham and her job had been to protect him. He now remembered how cool she had been when the pirates had attacked. Of course, she was used to dealing with such events. Eventually, Will drifted off to sleep.

Chapter Thirty-One

Mellnic had checked into a cheap hotel in the Notting Hill area. His primary concern was that the hotel had Wi-Fi. He had some spare clothes, a little cash, his phone and a pistol. His boss was in custody and his colleagues were all most likely dead. So he was on his own. He didn't have enough money to fly home and in any case, there wasn't much to fly home for, that was why he had arrived in the first place. He had lived quite comfortably with the others in North London, driving for his boss and doing the odd dubious assignment, which he didn't ask too many questions about, he got paid in cash, which he spent on fags, booze and the local women.

He sat on his bed and looked around at the depressing room. It reminded him a bit of the rooms he had escaped from in Eastern Europe. He scratched his head and thought. What information did he know that would help him get some money? He knew where his boss lived as he had picked him up and dropped him back home but thought that a visit there would be stupid as the cops would be crawling all over the place and any money would have been seized. He knew that the bloke in Sussex owed the boss money. Perhaps there was an angle there. What was his name? Mellnic tried to remember what his boss had said when the door burst open. What was it? Mellnic tried hard, but the name was missing from his memory. He had an idea. Surely, the shooting would be on the news. The room had an old small screen TV in the corner and Mellnic switched it on. What time was the news? Mellnic looked at his watch it read 4.30 p.m. He flicked through the channels but there was no news programme. He switched on to BBC One and lay back on the bed and watched some game show until the news came on at 6 p.m.

Mellnic had dozed off and suddenly came awake when he realised that the news had started. Some crisis in North Korea followed by some political discussions on Brexit. He wondered if Brexit would force him to go home. Mellnic was just thinking there would be nothing on the news about the shooting when the main presenter announced that there had been a major shooting incident and Mellnic immediately recognised the aerial camera shot of the house in Sussex. He recognised the drive and the swimming pool at the rear. He dragged the only chair in the room up close to the TV and turned up the sound. The aerial picture had now been replaced by a pretty looking woman, whose hair was blowing around and she kept removing stray strands from her face.

'Earlier this morning there was an incident at this house,' the reporter pointed over her shoulder at the front of the house but without turning away from the camera, 'in this quiet and rural part of Sussex, when the owner of the house, respected City lawyer, Sam Brewer, was gunned down in his own lounge following, what appears to have been an altercation between two gangs. One gang burst through the gates,' a shot of the very damaged gates was shown, 'followed by a second gang. Both gangs entered the house where many gunshots were fired and the police tell me there were at least three dead and one seriously injured in hospital. The police arrived before anyone had escaped and a number of arrests were made. It is not known how Mr Brewer was involved with these gangs or whether it was a case of mistaken identity. Mr Brewer's wife and young children are being looked after by friends tonight. This is Mellanie Tuckstall in Sussex.'

Mellnic switched off the TV as soon as the next news story started.

He now had the name he had wanted and googled Sam Brewer on his phone. There were a number of "Samuel Brewers" on Wikipedia but he spotted the one he was looking for from his picture. He had seen him standing in the hall, next to another man as the front door had burst open. He remembered the way Sam Brewer's expression had changed from surprise to anger and then to fear in seconds. He read on about his education, how he was married to a member of the aristocracy and that he was a partner in the solicitors firm of

116

Slater & Craig. Mellnic then googled the name Slater & Craig. He studied the faces of the four partners that were helpfully shown against their names down the right hand side of the firm's web site home page. He spotted Brewer immediately. There were three other pictures, one woman and two men. One of the pictures, he thought was probably the second man standing in the hall when Mellnic had burst open the front door. Will Slater was his name. It was likely that he was either now in a body bag or in hospital, following events at Brewer's home. So he would be no use to him. Mellnic ignored the woman and honed onto the third man – George Wright. He thought he was vaguely familiar but couldn't quite remember where he had seen him. Perhaps, he had been at the house too but he hadn't seen him coming out with the injured and the dead. It must have been somewhere else. He started to make a plan. The boss was expecting to receive some significant sums of money from Brewer. It was unlikely that he had received it on the last visit but perhaps someone else from his firm, say this George Wright, might know where it was and pay it direct to Mellnic, with a bit of persuasion. Mellnic checked the address of Slater & Craig from the website, checked the nearest tube station from a map on his phone and set off.

When Mellnic got to the office block that housed the firm of Slater & Craig, he strolled into the main downstairs foyer on a pretext of asking directions to the tube and noted that Slater & Craig's offices were on the third floor. There was a small café on the other side of the road and Mellnic made a plan.

Chapter Thirty-Two

Dawkin sat at his desk contemplating the Foundling murder. He had the papers from the file spread out in front of him. There weren't many. No motive, no suspect and no witnesses. Just a shadowy figure from a couple of nights before, who may or not be involved. However this was all about to change.

Sergeant Edgar knocked on Dawkin's half open door and came in.

'You will want to see this Gov,' said Edgar, plonking down a laptop onto Dawkin's desk.

'OK, what have you got?' asked Dawkin.

'Well, we looked at the CCTVs for the last week before the break in and nothing much apart from this man, who I think was checking out the camera positions.'

Dawkin peered at the fuzzy images on the screen.

'Even if we could recognise him, which we can't, we wouldn't get a conviction on this.'

'Correct,' said Edgar, 'but I thought I recognised him. Some mannerism, the way he walked, I don't know, something. So I thought the bloke would probably have come by car. So I did a sweep of the neighbouring streets where we had camera images and cross checked car registration numbers to the National Database and bingo!'

Dawkin looked at Edgar with his eyes wide open and a flicking gesture of his hand indicating that he wanted to know what Edgar had found out.

'One of the cars was registered to guess who?'

'If I knew Edgar, I wouldn't be sitting here listening to you rabbiting on, I would out there arresting him. Who, for fuck's sake?'

'Mr William Slater, no less,' replied Edgar with a smug smirk on his face.

'Really, that is interesting Edgar, well done,' said Dawkin leaning back in his chair and nodding his head. 'I knew there was something more about him but I couldn't just put my finger on it,' Dawkin said more to himself than Edgar.

'Shall we pick him up for questioning Gov?'

'Ummm, we have a slight problem here, Edgar. Slater is currently in hospital, he's been in a coma, I understand.'

'How do you know this, Gov?' asked Edgar.

'We were asked to put a "plod" outside his room in the hospital. Armed!'

'What happened, Gov?' asked Edgar.

'Don't know the detail but apparently a shoot up in Sussex with three dead, including Slater's business partner.'

'Cor, proper little merchant of death he is,' replied Edgar.

'Yea, anti-terrorist op apparently and 'ave had the Chief Super on the phone yesterday informing me that Slater is part of a much bigger operation that we can't "fuck up", his words not mine!'

'Blimey,' replied Edgar, 'you were right he was hiding something. Any idea what he is into Gov?'

'No, but it must be big and reckon it has come down from on high, way past the Chief Super,' replied Dawkin.

'So we do nothing then?' asked Edgar.

'I didn't say that. I gather Slater is now out of his coma, so I think I will pay him a visit and take some grapes,' said Dawkin with a wry smile on his face.

Chapter Thirty-Three

Will had a number of visitors during the next week in hospital, a couple of staff members from the office, both his partners, Sara and George, his doubles tennis partner from the club and Inspector Dawkin.

'Good morning, Mr Slater, how are you feeling?' asked Dawkin.

'Not too bad, thank you,' replied Will.

'You seem to be getting yourself into some interesting situations, Mr Slater!'

'Didn't think Sussex would have been your patch, too, Inspector.'

'It ain't but as you are still a suspect to Mr McCloud's murder and when I heard that you were poorly and in hospital I thought I would call and see how you were. Wouldn't want you dying on me now would I?'

'What, so you can pin Toby's murder on me.'

'Mr Slater,' said Dawkin, spreading his arms wide and lifting his shoulders in a mock gesture, 'as if I would.'

'Well, I don't know. How are the Police getting on with finding his murderer?'

'I think you would need to ask the Scottish Police that question but my understanding is that they think it was a professional hit, which, of course would rule you out. However, I am from the old school and never accept anything at face value, hence my visit.'

'Well, I think it has been a wasted visit Inspector. I am pretty much recovered and going home tomorrow and can't help you any further.'

'Never a wasted visit, Mr Slater,' said Dawkin. He was about to get up when he said, 'Oh I almost forgot. Do you know an accountant called Foundling?'

Will thought quickly, should he admit that he had been to his office? If he did he would then have to explain Java and the rest of the story. Although it was a dangerous game lying to the police, on this occasion he thought it was the best policy, at least for the present, until he could get straight in his mind, who was on his side and who wasn't.

'No,' replied Will pausing and then said, 'I don't think so,' pausing again, 'although my memory is still not fully functioning. If I do remember anything I will let you know.'

Dawkin raised his eyebrows in response.

'Ummm,' Dawkin replied signifying that he did not believe Will on either his loss of memory or that he would let Dawkin know if he did remember later.

'The problem is, Mr Slater, that Foundling was found murdered yesterday in his office. Are you sure we won't find any of your fingerprints?'

'If I have never been to his office, how could there be any fingerprints,' replied Will.

'Ummm' responded Dawkin again.

Dawkin got up and walked to the door and he then turned and said, 'I am sure our paths will cross again, Mr Slater, as there appear to be a number of loose ends in my investigation which I believe tie into you.'

Dawkin then quietly shut the door behind him.

Will sat in bed unnerved by the exchange. How much did Dawkin know about his visit to Foundling's office? He didn't touch anything when he broke in, as he wore gloves. What about when he visited earlier. In any case the cockney girl would be sure and recognise him.

Will felt tired and his head started to ache again. He would need to work out what to say to Dawkin, as Will was convinced that their paths would cross again, but he hadn't realised how soon that would be.

Chapter Thirty-Four

The next day the doctor popped into Will's room.

'Think you are OK to go home today as planned, but you must take it easy for a while. Your body will let you know when you can get back to your normal routine. The nurse will bring you your medications to take away and then you can go.'

Will thanked the doctor and shook his hand.

Will eased himself out of bed and put on the clothes that he had arrived in from the ambulance. His shirt and jacket were bloodstained and both had holes from the bullet. Will put his finger through the hole in his jacket and reflected on the events that had caused it. His jacket seemed heavy and as he put his hand into the side pocket he realised that he still had the gun taken from Toby's house. He then felt for the envelope containing the list of numbers that he had also taken. That was still there too. He was sure that this was important and was probably the list that Sam Brewer had said had been stolen, but he didn't quite know why or what it meant. He put the envelope back in his pocket and finished getting dressed.

After he had been given his meds with various instructions, Will made his way down to the main hospital reception to get a cab.

The taxi driver on his way home was one of the talkative types. Will reckoned black cab drivers fell into two categories, those surly ones who purveyed the image that they were doing you a favour by taking you to your destination and the talkative ones who either knew how to resolve every problem in the world or thought you would and asked for your views.

This cabbie looked at Will in his mirror, saw the bandages, bruises and blood on his clothes.

'Cor, mate you look as if you have been in Iraq or Afghanistan,' and roared with laughter at his own comment. 'I did a bit of time as a squaddie so I know a bullet hole when I sees one. The head looks pretty ugly, too. What, you got signed off medically?' enquired the driver.

Will thought he would play along with the driver.

'No, I actually got this in Sussex dealing with some rough boys.'

'Cor strewth, mate, what is the country coming to. I hope they got them bastards that did that to you.'

'Yea, well, a couple of them are dead now,' replied Will.

'Wow,' replied the driver looking carefully at Will in his mirror and deciding that perhaps he would just drive for the rest of the journey.

With the conversation at an end Will closed his eyes and dozed off until the cab reached his home.

Will opened his front door and realised that his cleaner had been in whilst he had been in hospital as there was a neat pile of mail and junk circulars on the hall table just inside the front door. The house smelled clean but a bit airless from being shut up.

Will felt still pretty fragile and the bullet wound was still very sore as he moved around opening windows to let some air in.

He took off his jacket and hung it on the back of his study chair. He went into the kitchen made himself a pot of coffee and took the cup upstairs where he showered and changed into clean clothes, putting his blood stained items in a pile for the refuse and the rest into the basket for washing.

Will poured himself another cup of coffee, took a couple of painkillers and went into his study and sat at his desk. He took out the sheet of paper and the gun and laid them on the desk in front of him.

He examined the gun first. He was careful as he didn't want it to go off. He examined the safety catch and worked out which was on and which was off. With it off he pressed a button on the handle and the magazine slid down. Will pulled it out. It was full of bullets. He had seen in films that there was probably also a bullet in the gun ready for firing but he wasn't sure how to get that out without pulling the trigger, so he slid the magazine back into the handle and laid the gun back on the table. It was a criminal offense to be in the possession of a handgun, in fact any gun, without a licence and licences were not issued for handguns unless they were for sporting purposes. Will now wondered why he had picked it up as he was not sure how he would get rid of it safely.

He now looked again at the sheet of paper. Five lines, each containing eight numbers. They reminded him of bank account numbers and would fit in with the comments made by Sam. He then had a thought. He needed to look at the schedules that he had photocopied at Foundling's offices. All the papers were in his briefcase, which was in his car, presumably still in Sam's drive. He made a mental note to ask the police if he could pick it up. His mobile phone was still in his pocket so he sent the schedules that he had photographed at Foundling's office to his e-mail account again and printed them off from a printer in the corner of his study.

The schedule he was looking for listed all of Java PLC's bank accounts. There were five separate accounts and all at the same bank based in the Virgin Islands. That was where the supposed owners of Java had registered their address, although there was no doubt in Will's mind that the owners would certainly be living somewhere else. Possibly, even in London. Helpfully, the scheduled listed the address of the bank and a contact name.

Will looked at his watch. The bank's time zone would be a few hours behind UK time so their offices should now be open. Will Googled the address and noted down the telephone number on the photocopied schedule. Will sat back and considered what he would say to the bank. There was sure to be some password which he didn't have and it might require a personal visit to the bank to make any transfers. The question was how was he to find out? He had learnt early in life when negotiating deals that if you were confident and appeared sure of your position, then often that was enough to get what you needed. Will picked up the phone and dialled the telephone number.

'Hello, First National how can we help you?' came the reply from the dialled number.

'Good morning, can I speak to Mr Justerini, the manager, please?' asked Will.

'May I say who is calling?'

'My name is Will Slater and am a client of your bank,' replied Will.

'Just a moment, please, sir.' And then after a brief pause, 'Putting you through, sir.'

'Justerini,' a voice said in an American accent.

'Mr Justerini, this is Will Slater of Java PLC, I hope you remember me?' Will was assuming that all the accounts had been opened up using his name as the only director of Java.

'Mr Slater, of course, although we have never met, how can I forget the clear access instructions to your accounts. How can I help you?'

Well that was useful and more information than Will could have hoped for in the opening gambit. Perhaps this chap was not as bright as his title might indicate.

'As it has been a few years since I opened the accounts,' this was evident from the length of time Java had been operating, 'I just wanted to check that the arrangements were still in place in case I had to move funds in the near future. Can we just go through the details and passwords requirements that you have noted against the accounts just in case you were, say, not available, when a transaction had to take place.'

'I think my unavailability would be highly unlikely, Mr Slater, but I suppose it pays to be cautious with such large sums of money. Were you expecting to make any transfers shortly?' asked Justerini.

'No, no, the business is going well, but we may have to change accountants and thought that this was a good opportunity to check everything was in good order.'

'Quite so, Mr Slater, let's have a look. Ah, Foundling is the accountant per the accounts I have on file. Is there something wrong?'

'Unfortunately, Mr Foundling has had to take early retirement,' replied Will but not with any amusement in his voice as Will had been very near to early retirement himself a few times recently, too.

'OK, let's have a look at the notes on the file. These are all as stipulated by you in an e-mail dated,' there was a pause, Will assumed, while Justerini was flicking through screen files looking for the e-mail. '2014, that's it, January 2014.'

'Perfect,' said Will, 'and those instructions are clearly noted on the file?'

'There most certainly are,' replied Justerini.

'Just to be clear could you, please, just read the notes to make sure that they have been entered correctly?' asked Will.

'We cannot afford to make mistakes like that here, Mr Slater, but, of course, I will check. The file states '*A transfer has to be done in person by either you or an authorised representative and they must have the 8 number account codes that only you and I have and for extra security each account has a final different letter which can only be disclosed in person.*'

'Excellent, Mr Justerini, quite correct. I am glad my funds are in such safe hands. Thank you.'

'Absolute pleasure, Mr Slater, and if we can help with any transfers please let me know.'

'Will do, bye for now,' replied Will.

'Goodbye, Mr Slater and have a good day.'

Will put down the phone. Had he been in Justerini's office, he would have seen the manager unlock his top desk drawer and remove a piece of paper. His instructions were given to him when the account was first opened. Should he receive any communications in connection with Java's bank accounts then he was to call the two telephone numbers that had been given to him. Justerini had the impression that the first number was the person operating the account and the second number was the overall owner. Justerini picked up the phone and made the two calls. The second number went to an unidentifiable voicemail.

Will rocked back in his chair thinking about how he was going to work out the final letters for the code. This seemed to be the missing link and was sure that this piece of paper was what everyone had been looking for. He popped the gun and the paper back in his jacket pocket.

Will felt very tired, he switched on the television for background noise and settled down on the sofa for a nap. He woke up three hours later. The house was completely dark, even the TV had switched itself off and for a moment he couldn't work out where he was. He got up, switched on some lights and poured himself a whisky. He hadn't eaten for a while but didn't feel like doing any cooking. Having looked through the freezer for a ready meal, nothing appealed to him so Will decided to have cheese on toast. He poured himself another whisky and pondered on his next step. When he finished his supper, Will still felt tired, so he had another couple of painkillers and went to bed.

Chapter Thirty-Five

Will was still tired and sore when he awoke the following morning. After a very hot shower to try and ease away some of the stiffness in his body, he made fresh coffee, devoured another couple of painkillers and sat down in his study to consider his next move. He removed the sheet of numbers from his jacket pockets and laid it out on his desk. He hadn't been sitting down long when the doorbell rang. He looked at his watch and wondered who would be calling so relatively early in the morning.

He got up and answered the door to find Sara Crombie, one of his partners outside.

'Can I come in, please?' she asked.

'Of course, how nice of you to come around.'

Will was just closing the door behind Sara when another figure appeared pushing the door open.

'Yer, good to see you too,' the figure said. It was Sara's husband, Peter, looking as aggressive as always, the colour of his complexion matching his fiery red hair.

Will looked surprised, even more so when Peter pulled a gun from his pocket and waved it in Will's face.

'You have something that belongs to me and I want it now.'

'What are you talking about and how dare you come in threatening me. I am going to call the police.'

But before Will had time to move, Peter hit Will in the face with the side of the pistol.

'Shit, shit,' cried Will as he bent over holding his face in his hands as a dribble of blood seeped through his fingers.

'Why did you do that, you bastard?' mumbled Will through his hands. 'I have just come out of hospital with serious injuries.'

'Because you are an interfering arsehole and your usefulness has come to an end. You should have been left well alone. I want what belongs to me, the page of numbers that McCloud gave you.'

Will straightened himself up.

'I haven't got any numbers,' he replied.

Peter raised the barrel of the pistol again.

'OK, OK,' Will said holding up his hands in surrender, 'it is in the study. I will get it for you.'

'I am right behind you, so nothing funny mate,' invoked Peter.

Will was scared, extremely angry and in a good deal of pain. He could see no reason why Peter would let him live now that he had disclosed himself. He had to act fast. Then he realised what he had to do. He would only get one chance at this so he had to make sure first time.

'The sheet is in my jacket pocket,' said Will bending over his study chair making sure Peter couldn't see what he was doing.

'Wait, this looks like it on the desk,' exclaimed Peter, stretching his left hand to pick up the sheet and momentarily pointing the gun away from Will. It was all Will needed, he pulled the gun out of his jacket pocket, flicked the safety catch off and said, 'Drop your gun, Peter, or I will shoot you.'

Peter turned looking surprised. Will already knew he was going to have to shoot Peter so his finger was already tightening on the trigger.

'You haven't the guts to pull that trigger, however I don't need you anymore and I have the guts.'

Will remembered hearing that when tumultuous events happen everything seems to move in slow motion, like being involved in a car crash. At that moment, he could see the sneer on Peter's face and Peter's finger squeezing the trigger and then the bang.

Peter's face changed from a sneer to one of surprise and almost incongruity as he looked at his shoulder which was a mass of torn flesh and bone, his right arm hanging limply by his side. As if in slow motion his knees folded and he fell to the floor screaming in agony.

Sara, who had been standing at the door, watching the events unfold and before Will could grab her, flew across the room to Peter's side picking up the gun that had slid out of his hand and shouting out loud, 'I am so sorry, Will, I should never have allowed this to happen, he is a mad bastard.' Sara backed away to the study door.

And for the second time in as many seconds Will heard the ominous bang. But this time not from the gun he was holding.

Will looked down in disbelief as Peter made the last twitch of the dying as the blood oozed from a jagged hole through his head. Sara had killed her own husband.

'He was a mad and evil bastard,' she cried, 'someone should have done this sooner.'

Will stood there for a few minutes as Sara collapsed to the floor and wept uncontrollably, lying over Peter's body.

Will reached down and removed the gun, lifting it by the barrel and placing this and his gun on the desk.

He then helped Sara up and led her through the front door where they sat on the front door step. Will dialled 999, explained that there had been a shooting and that there was a dead victim, and waited for the cavalry to arrive.

'I should have married you, Will, not that heinous man,' sobbed Sara. 'I can't understand what got into him, he was obsessed by the money from all his crooked deals. I tried to persuade him to give himself up before it was too late. He insisted on me coming today and threatened to kill me as well as you if I didn't. I thought that perhaps if I came I could at least protect you in some way but...'

Sara's short soliloquy was interrupted by the sound of numerous sirens. The first to arrive were the Armed Response Unit.

'Armed police, on your knees with your hands behind your head,' screamed a huge menacing looking policeman wearing the customary Kevlar bulletproof vest and pointing some type of machine pistol at Will and Sara.

Three other officers spread out in a fan.

'Who dialled 999?' screamed the policeman again.

'I did, we are unarmed, the victim is inside and the guns are on the desk,' replied Will.

The policeman indicated silently to the other three officers, who entered the house in a crouching style, while he continued to point his gun at Will and Sara.

After a few minutes, one of the officers appeared at the front door.

'All clear,' he said.

By now the road outside the house was full of various emergency service vehicles. The next people to arrive were the paramedics, which Will could have told them was a waste of time. Then, low and behold, walking up the drive in a nonchalant "know it all" attitude was none other than Inspector Dawkin and hurrying behind trying to keep up with Dawkin's large strides was Sergeant Edgar.

'Well, well, well Mr Slater,' said Dawkin with a grin on his face, 'this should be an interesting story. Cuff them both, Edgar, and take them to the station.'

Edgar read them their rights and both were hustled off into separate police cars and driven off for questioning.

Chapter Thirty-Six

When Will arrived at the police, he asked for a legal representative to be present before he was interviewed.

'Got plenty to hide, Mr Slater?' asked Dawkin.

'No, but just think it makes sense in these circumstances,' replied Will.

Dawkin gave his customary 'Ummmm'.

Will called one of his solicitor friends, Carl Lessan, who specialised in criminal law, to act as his representative. While waiting Will asked for a doctor to look at the wound on his face and for more painkillers.

Eventually, Will and his solicitor were escorted into an interview room. After the formalities and the switching on of the tape recording machine, Dawkin started.

'Let's see, Mr Slater, where should we start? Murder, attempted murder, an accomplice to murder, grievous bodily harm, manslaughter, possession of an illegal weapon and burglary. I think that should do for starters. I am going to throw the book at you, Mr Slater.'

'I think that comment is quite unnecessary, Inspector, my client is a respectable man and not some low life criminal that you obviously normally deal with,' said Carl Lessan.

'That's OK Carl, I will deal with this,' interjected Will, 'I think you will find that there is no evidence of murder, attempted murder or GBH, I wounded Peter Crombie in self-defence. I couldn't stop Sara from killing her husband and am sure she will confirm that in her statement. I hold up my hands to the possession of an illegal weapon,' said Will putting his hands upwards in a surrender mode, 'but know nothing about any burglary.'

'I am not talking about the murder of Crombie, Mr Slater, I am talking about the murders of Foundling and McCloud,' said Dawkin.

'This is ridiculous, Inspector, you have arrested my client in connection with the events at his home today and not in connection with any other incidents for which I doubt that you have any evidence to hold my client,' said Lessan, 'he has admitted to the possession of a firearm but with someone of my client's good character, he will only get a suspended sentence. So we need get real here and suggest that we get my client in front of a magistrate as soon as possible to enable bail to be obtained.'

'Not so fast, I want to know why Mr Slater's car was photographed in the vicinity of Foundling's offices a few days before he was murdered?' asked Dawkin.

Lessan laughed out loud.

'Come on, Inspector, we were not born yesterday, you are going to have to do better than that and if that is the only bit of evidence you have on my client in connection with the murder of Foundling then you are not going to get very far.'

'We will see, I haven't finished with your client in connection with this murder yet. Mr Slater, you told me you had never been to Foundler's office, yet his secretary recognised you from a picture we showed her. Apparently you visited Foundler the day before the burglary.'

'Yes,' replied Will, 'but that was during my stay in hospital and I did say that my memory was hazy.'

'Ummm, but why were you there Mr Slater?' replied Dawkin.

'His firm were accountants to a company that I was interested in,' replied Will.

'Did you obtain the information that you wanted?' asked Dawkin.

'Yes and no,' Will replied.

'OK, Inspector,' cut in Lessan, 'I haven't heard anything concrete so far and think this is really a fishing trip.'

'Ummm,' replied Dawkin.

There was a knock from outside and a uniformed officer put his head around the interview room door.

'A call for you, Inspector.'

'Can't you see I am busy, I will call back.'

The uniformed office shuffled from one foot to the other and was obviously not going to leave the room.

'I am to tell you Inspector, that it is urgent and it can't wait,' said the officer.

Dawkin slapped his hand on the desk, glared at the uniformed office and slowly got up.

'I haven't finished yet,' he said as he left the room continuing to glare but this time at Will and his solicitor.

Edgar said to the recording machine, 'Inspector Dawkin has left the interview.'

Lessan looked at Will and raised his eyebrows. They sat in silence for about ten minutes, when suddenly the door open with huge gusto and Dawkin walk in and from the door he said, 'It grieves me to say this but you are free to leave, Mr Slater. You obviously have friends in high places but I find it totally unacceptable when a criminal act goes unpunished, so I can assure you that I am going to try my damnest to make sure that you do not go unpunished, but at the moment I can do nothing to keep you here, so I suggest you get out of my sight quickly,' and with that Dawkin turned and stomped out of the interview room.

Will looked at Lessan and this time he raised his eyebrows. Lessan shuffled his papers together, picked them up, put them in his briefcase and indicated to Will that they should leave.

Edgar showed them out and headed back to Dawkin's office.

'What happened, Gov?' asked Edgar.

Dawkin was so angry he could hardly speak.

'Bloody SO 15, Slater is too important to others for us to arrest him. I am not going to rest until I get that bastard for something.'

Chapter Thirty-Seven

Will and Lessan sat in Lessan's car outside the police station.

'Well, what happened there Will?' asked Lessan.

'Haven't a clue, Carl.'

'Come on, Will you must know something,' pressed Lessan.

'Well, I know SO 15 are snooping all over this case and it is to do with terrorism. I think Crombie was one of the main suspects.' Will then gave Lessan a brief synopsis of the conversation with Allan and how it seemed to fit in with the deaths of McCloud and Foundling. He also admitted to his night time sauté into Foundling's office.

'Bloody hell, Will! What have you got yourself into?'

'To be honest, Carl, there was no one I could trust, and still isn't. I need to find the answers to this by myself. Dawkin thinks I have killed all these people, SO 15 won't tell him anything, so I have to work it out myself. Who is behind this whole enterprise and why they are framing me. When I do, well, then, I will need you to protect me, I don't trust Allan either as when he has what he wants, who is to say he won't just throw me to Dawkin so the case can be closed?'

'Yes, I can see you are in a very difficult position,' said Lessan thoughtfully. 'I am going to drive you home but I want you to keep me informed at every turn and don't hesitate to call me anytime, day or night.'

'Thanks, Carl, much appreciated and send me your bill for today,' responded Will.

The police had all left Will's house and the only indication that it had recently been a crime scene was a piece of blue police tape attached to the side of the porch that was flapping in the breeze. Will snatched the tape, pulled it off the porch, rolled in a ball and tossed it into the front garden as a sign of irritation to the whole event.

Will entered his house and wondered if he could continue to live there knowing that someone had been killed in his study. Although the police had cleared up a lot of the blood, there were still stains on the carpet. He stood there staring at the carpet, remembering the events as they had unfolded earlier in the day. Will made a mental note to phone a carpet shop the next day and for them to measure up and replace it.

It was now late, so Will made himself a sandwich, poured himself a glass of wine and went up to bed.

The next day Will woke early and made a decision about what he was going to do. He phoned George Wright, before he had left home for the office. Although George was not entirely happy with what Will was suggesting, Will was the senior partner, had the largest share and George thought was probably not worth arguing about.

Will drove to the office and gathered the whole team in the general office and sitting on the edge of one of the desks, he explained.

'This has been a very difficult time for us all and I appreciate the way all of you have maintained a very professional approach to the dealings with our clients. George and I are now the only remaining partners of Slater & Craig and we don't really think it is practical for us to continue. There are a lot of questions that will need to be answered in connection with the death of Sam and it is likely that Sara will get a long custodial sentence, so I think the firm's reputation is finished. Therefore, we have decided,' turning to look at George, 'that regrettably the only course of action is to cease the business. I want to do this in an orderly manner so none of our clients and none of you suffer unduly.

'So, this is my plan; I want all those who are client facing to draw up a list of the state of play of the work you are doing and an estimate of what has to be done to complete current assignments, who has to do what and how long you estimate it will take. I would like to see you all individually to go through your lists after lunch, this should allow you time to do the exercise. I will instruct the accounts department to double everyone's salaries from the beginning of last month and will pay a bonus of a year's salary to everyone who does not leave until their final client matter is resolved. For administration staff, I will also double salaries and pay a year's salary as a bonus to everyone who leaves at the time agreed by me and which seems reasonably bearing in mind the need to continue to run the office. For many I would like to think that will be the last day of operation of the firm. I hope you think that is reasonable and, of course, we will allow time off for interviews for new positions but please give me as much notice as possible so we can deal with clients correctly and not put too much pressure on those who remain until the end. If you have any questions or would like to speak with me in private, please, do so. Thank you for listening.'

Will continued to sit on the edge of the desk waiting for any questions. There was some shuffling of feet and a few looks between members of the team until one of the solicitors spoke.

'Will, thank you for your honesty and for your generous offer. From what I understand, you have been set up and are innocent of any accusations made against you and I for one am happy to continue working for you until there is nothing more to do.'

There was then a chorus of 'Yes, and me' and 'I agree'.

'Thank you for your support and confidence,' replied Will, 'so let's get to it.' Will stood up and went into his office.

George followed Will into his office.

'Well, that is that then,' said George. 'Any idea what you are going to do?'

'No, not at the moment. I suspect there will be some court appearances and am not off the hook for either McCloud's or Foundling's murders yet. So am going to have to see how that pans out, too. I need to concentrate on that as a priority. It would be good if you can check on how the client work is winding down, please.'

'Of course,' said George.

'And what about you? I know I have sprung it on you but what will you do?' asked Will.

'You know I haven't got a clue. I am not sure I want to stay in the profession. Perhaps try something completely new. I have money so that gives me some opportunities,' replied George.

Will nodded and George, seeing that this was the end of the conversation, went back to his room.

After a series of meetings with his team during the afternoon, Will estimated that the outstanding cases should all be completed within the next three or four months.

He then went through the firm's finances with his head of finance, confirming the agreed changes to the salaries and instructing a provision to be made for the likely bonuses. He asked that a provisional profit and loss account to be produced so he could make interim profit payments to Sam's estate and was sure that Sara's children would need support.

Will felt pleased that he had set out a plan to wind down the firm but realised that he felt very tired so decided that it was time to go home.

Chapter Thirty-Eight

Will had just opened a bottle of South African Pinotage, his favourite red wine, put a ready meal in the microwave when the front door bell rang. He really didn't feel like any company and was tempted to not answer but it rang again, not a long aggressive ring, but a short friendly ring. Will remembered what had happened the last time he had had an unsolicited caller and opened the door on the chain. Standing under the porch light was Jay.

'Hi, can I come in?' she said slightly tilting her head to one side.

Will nodded, released the chain on the door and let her in.

She took her coat off and smiled at Will.

'How are you? I have heard all the news and wanted to come over to check that you were still all in one piece,' she said with a smile.

As always, she looked stunning even in a simple button shirt and tight jeans. Will realised, again, that he was not "over" her even after all the events that had occurred and some he still levelled at her.

'Not too, bad thanks,' and after a short pause, 'it is good to see you again.' He reached out and gave her a hug.

'Would you like a glass of wine, I have just poured myself one?'

'That would be great, thanks, Will.'

The microwave chirped to let Will know that his meal was ready.

'Have you eaten?' he asked Jay.

'Not yet, but I will get something when I get home, you go ahead and eat.'

'No, I hate eating alone. I will put another dish into the microwave. It won't take long and we can have the second glass while we wait.' He smiled remembering the countless bottles they had shared together and only such a very short time ago.

'Spagbol, OK? Goes very well with the Pinotage,' Will said and laughed.

'Not the other way around then,' replied Jay and also laughed.

They sat opposite each other at the kitchen table and both started to speak at the same time.

'Sorry, you go first.'

'No, you.'

'I would have come before,' said Jay, 'but my boss thought it would be inappropriate given the circumstances and he was not sure whether you were completely innocent or putting on a good act.'

'And what did you think?' asked Will.

'Harry is a good judge of character, but I told him that I was convinced that you were not involved, but he thought that because of our relationship, my view was not totally objective.'

'So, was the relationship part of the plan from the start?' asked Will.

'No, certainly not. Officers are not supposed to get involved with their cases in that way. In fact, it is very difficult for officers to get involved romantically at all. As Paul, my husband, was away so much on active service, it didn't seem too much of a problem and we had agreed that when he left the forces, we would both move somewhere completely away. But, of course, that all changed when he was killed,' Jay looked down and pursed her bottom lip. 'That was a while ago now as you know.'

'So, what was true and what was made up from all that you said to me. Your family, background etc.'

'Everything was true. I have a daughter, who lives with my parents and the rest is all work.'

'And us, was that all fake or a passing fad?'

'That is partly why I have come to see you. I intend to leave the service. My parents are not getting any younger and they need a life as retired people, not running my daughter hither and thither. That should be my job. Anyway, a daughter should have at least one parent living with them,' Jay paused.

'I, also, wanted to say that my feelings for you were, are, not faked.' Jay looked directly into Will's eyes. 'This is difficult for me as I know you feel I have betrayed you. If at all possible, I would like to be part of your life going forward and you mine. I know it is a lot to ask but I had to say it as it is very important to me and if I didn't get your answer I would always feel that I had cheated myself,' Jay now looked down, 'the thing is,' Jay paused again, 'the thing is, I think that I have fallen in love with you, Will.'

Will leant back in his chair.

'Wow,' he said puffing out his lips. 'That was some speech.'

The microwave chirped again and both ignored it.

Jay poured some more wine into her glass and looked across at Will who was just staring at her across the table.

'Please, say something, Will,' pleaded Jay, 'I just need to know and then I will leave you forever if that is what you want.'

'I am closing down the firm and intend to do something else in the future. I haven't a clue what or where, therefore making any commitment by either of us before this is all over would be a mistake, however my feelings for you are still the same but feel very sore mentally and physically. I don't want you to leave but I need more time to think everything through. However,' said Will, wagging a finger in the air and looking down at his empty glass, 'I do expect my guests to offer to fill my glass before refilling theirs.'

For a moment Jay looked stunned and when she saw a huge smile on Will's face she jumped up and rushed around the table and they grabbed each other. Tears were running down both of their faces.

'I can wait as long as you like,' replied Jay through sobs of happiness. 'I am so happy,' cried Jay, 'I wasn't sure what you would say. I hope and prayed that you would take me back.'

Will bent down and kissed Jay on the lips. He smiled and took her hand and led her towards the stairs.

'I am not hungry anymore and I can think of something I would rather do.'

Jay looked at Will and nodded and headed upstairs.

Chapter Thirty-Nine

Will woke early the next morning and almost thought he had dreamt the last evening but saw Jay beside him sleeping. He got out of bed quietly and went down stairs and made a fresh pot of coffee. He sat in the conservatory and wondered what he should do next. He decided he needed two brains rather than one and took up another cup to his bedroom for Jay. He kissed her gently on the forehead.

'Wake up, sleepy head, we have to make some plans.'

Jay stretched.

'This is no way to treat a girl. First you take advantage of me, several times, during the night and then wake me up early to discuss what you are going to do today,' grumbled Jay smiling throughout.

'Yes, but at least I have brought you a cup of coffee.'

Jay sat up in bed pulling the duvet up to cover her body.

'So what are you thinking, lover boy.'

'I have few questions that need sorting out first. When did you start "watching over me"? Did you see what happened in Michael Bore's villa? How did my attacker really die? I don't really buy the police's story that he fell and hit his head. I also saw a car in the drive that had disappeared by the time I returned from making my statement to the police. I now wonder whether this was something to do with you,' asked Will.

Jay replied, 'I had already been assigned to watch you and protect you. Allan was convinced that you were the way to get to the ringleader and although he didn't really care about you, per se, he recognised that if you were dead, the trail would go cold. So, my job was to protect you. I was on the same plane to Palma and followed you to the villa. Alone, I could not watch you twenty-four hours a day. We thought that the villa was probably secure and via Interpol we persuaded the security company to let us know if they were any breaches of the alarm or panic calls made. When they got your call that night I was informed immediately. As I was only staying around the corner in a small hotel I was able to get to the villa before them.

Chapter Forty

Jay got the call from the security company to say that the panic alarm had been triggered and the occupant had said there was an intruder in the villa. Jay had only got partly undressed so she only had to pull on jeans and shoes and rush down to her hired car and drive the few hundred yards to the villa and park in the road. The front of the villa looked all shut up, so she suspected that the intruder would have entered from the rear. At the side of the villa was a high gate to let maintenance people into the grounds. Too high and too smooth to scale without help. She sprinted back to her car and drove it up to the side gate. She then climbed onto the roof and with a leap was able to get a handhold on top of the gate. She climbed up and half slid and half jumped down the other side. She realised that she would need to find another way out of the villa.

She crouched down and waited for her eyes to become accustomed to the environment around. She had expected everything to be dark but the garden and pool area lights had been left on so she was able to see quite clearly. She needed a weapon as she was not allowed to carry her gun onto Spanish soil. On the next tier below the swimming pool was a hut tucked into the corner of the garden. She approached this in a crouched run. It was not locked. However, there was no light in here. She removed her phone from the pocket of the cargo pants she was wearing and switched on the torch app. Immediately, she spotted her weapon. A small-headed hammer, probably used for putting plant stakes into the dry ground. Armed and ready for action she retraced her steps back to the villa. She could now hear sirens and guessed that the security and police had almost arrived and she hoped she was not too late to save her ward. She crouch ran up the steps to the pool area and stopped in the shadows made by the lights. From the villa, she heard a cry and then two shots. *Damn*, she thought, *whoever is in there is armed*, and looked down at her poultry weapon. She was just about to leave her hiding spot, when above her, one of the doors to what she assumed was the main living area of the villa slid open and she saw a man came out. This did not look like the man she was protecting and he was clearly in pain and was limping badly and as he approached one of the patio lights, Jay noticed that there was blood coming out of his left shoe. She also noticed that he held a gun in his right hand. Jay moved forward to meet the man from his right side so he would have no room to point the gun at her.

Jay moved forward in the shadows to the base of the steps coming down from the terrace above and as the man hobbled down from the last step, Jay realised that he had changed hands with the gun, which made it possible for him to hold the rail down the steps. He heard Jay at the last moment and started to swing the gun towards her. She had planned to smash the attacker's right wrist with her hammer forcing him to drop his weapon but now she could not reach the left wrist so instead of a downward blow, she flicked the hammer upwards catching the man heavily on the side of his head.

For a moment, the attacker looked stunned, grunted and collapsed in a heap at the foot of the steps. Jay kicked the loosened gun from his hand, but the attacker looked very still. She felt for a pulse and realised that her blow had been harder than she had wanted as the man was dead. This was not good news as she didn't want to highlight her presence. She got hold of the man under the arms and with some difficulty managed to drag him to the edge of a small plant bed to the side of the pool which had large rocks to demarcate the bed from the poolside floor tiles. She picked up one of the rocks and banged it against the victim's head in the same spot as the hammer had struck. She then rolled the man onto his right side with his head against the now replaced and bloody rock. Hopefully, from a cursory look from a policeman in the early hours of the morning, it would look as if he had slipped and hit his head.

Probably not a scenario that would stand up to a lot of scrutiny, but she hoped the Spanish police would accept what they saw at face value. She now had to work out how to get out through the villa. The sirens had stopped but she could see the blue light flashing in the night sky from the other side of the villa. She hid back in the shadows to wait her opportunity. She wiped the handle of the hammer with her T-shirt and rubbed the head with the blood in a patch of soil in the flowerbed in the shadows where she was hiding. She was right beside a hedge which separated the villa from the one next door. She pushed the hammer as far as she could into the hedge and reckoned that it was hidden from casual inspection. She now heard voices from the villa and to her relief she could hear an English voice, so her ward had survived. Then two armed policemen came out of the same terrace door as the attacker and with a torch appeared to be following the trail of blood from the victim. It didn't take them long to find his body. Their assessment of his health seemed to agree with hers and although one of the policeman made a half-hearted search of the grounds with his torch, you could see that they were satisfied that they had found the intruder and that their immediate job was done.

Jay waited in the shadows for another hour, during which time, the body of the attacker was removed. Eventually, all the police movements and voices died down and the blue flashing ceased to light up the night sky. Jay cautiously made her way up the steps to the terrace below the one from where everyone had exited down the steps. The glass door of the middle room, which she assumed was one of the bedrooms had shattered and she stepped through and listened. She heard nothing but more importantly her keen senses noted no other presence. She left the bedroom. All was in darkness, so she risked the torch on her phone again and found the stairs at the end of the corridor. She turned off the torch and listened again and sensed no one. She reached the top of the stairs and switched on her phone torch again. With a quick sweep she noticed the trail of blood and more importantly the front door. She opened the door a fraction and peeped out but there was no one outside. She rescued her car and drove back to her hotel to catch a few hours' sleep and to work out what to do next to protect her ward.

Will had been lying back in the bed listening to Jay's story. When she finished, he sat up and said, 'Remind me not to mess around with you. I have another question for you. Do you know what happened when I went up to Toby's house the second time. Were you there too?'

'Yes, the story went like this,' said Jay.

Chapter Forty-One

Jay waited in line in her black Range Rover, three cars behind Will. She watched the policeman move down the line of vehicles speaking to each driver in turn. When the policeman got to Will, she noted him gesticulating to the logging lorry further up the line. When the policeman reached her car, she showed him her identity badge and asked him what he had said to the Subaru driver. He turned to check which car she was referring to and told her that he had allowed him to continue provided he followed the logging truck. She explained that it was essential to national security that she got in front of the Subaru. The policeman thought for a second and nodded. He indicated that Jay could leave the queue and proceed but with caution. Jay pulled out and took the right turn at the junction up towards Ballachulish.

The road was difficult as the snow had just started falling again and even with the weight of the Range Rover and its four-wheel drive, she never felt she had full control on any of the bends. She kept looking in her rear-view mirror and saw the logging lorry also pull out of the line of vehicles but soon she could see nothing behind and not much in front. She just concentrated on the road and made sure she got to Ballachulish before Will. At least Will would have the tracks of the logging lorry to follow, she thought, as she saw the white out poles in front of her peeking out of the whiteness. It was impossible to determine between the sky and the land. It was just all white. She couldn't do more than 20 miles an hour for fear of missing the next set of whiteout poles. She had to concentrate so hard she felt a headache coming on. Whenever she thought she was on a straight stretch of road, she looked into her mirror, as her next concern was that the logging lorry would be going faster and might not see her until too late. Occasionally, a light cloud passed and she could see a little further both forward and in her mirror. In one of those passing moments, she thought she caught sight of the lorry still quite some way behind. As she ascended into Glen Coe, the clouds suddenly parted and were replaced by brilliant sunshine, the glare was so strong that it made her headache much worse but she could now see the lorry and it was making good time. She felt that, had the clouds and snow been around for any longer, that lorry would have been up her backside.

Jay pushed on through the Glen and down to Ballachulish, turning right towards Toby McCloud's house. Jay noticed from the tracks that there had been a car up the road before her. She passed McCloud's house on the right and from the virgin snow in the drive she could see no one had approached the house that way. A little further up Jay spotted a small car tucked into the side of the road. There was no one in it and she drove on and parked a few yards further on. She took her pistol out of the glove compartment and slipped it into her shoulder holster. She got out of the car put on her parka, took out a map and leant against the boot pretending to examine the map but watching and listening, using her senses to see if she could establish the whereabouts of the driver of the other car. If the driver of the car was going to do some harm and he wasn't in the grounds of the house, Jay assumed he would need high ground to fire off a shot. Jay looked around and the only place would be up the bank on the opposite side of the road from the house. Taking her map and looking like a hiker, she started to walk along the road towards the house examining the map regularly as if she was looking for a footpath. She was looking for footprints in the snow. After a few yards and close to the other car she saw where the driver had climbed the embankment. She looked around again as if examining her options and then strode off in the same direction as the driver up the bank. It was an easy climb and the footprints were still clear. Jay then heard another car in the distant, which she assumed was Will. Jay hurried on but the snow was thick and she couldn't afford to let the driver know she was there. She heard Will's car crunching the snow and ice towards McCloud's house. She heard Will's car come to a halt and the engine switched off. Then, to her horror, she heard three shots ring out, she pulled her gun from its holster and hurried on still following the footprints. She was getting close to the edge of the bank so she crouched down and peered through the lower branches of the trees. As the shooter hadn't moved, Jay thought that he must have missed with his first few shots so she had to get to him before he could shoot again. She carefully took another two steps forward and peered again. This time Jay could see a pair of legs lying prone in the snow. She eased herself into a better position, so she could see the shooter fully. Holding the gun in front of her in the extended arm shooting position, she stepped out behind the shooter.

'Freeze, I am armed,' called out Jay.

The shooter rolled over quickly leaving his rifle lying in the snow but with a pistol in his hand. Jay shot first and didn't miss. Jay crouched over the shooter to make sure he was dead. She searched his pockets, but they were all empty apart from car keys. Lying low, she looked over the edge of the bank towards the house and saw Will was apparently manoeuvring his car to provide cover to the front door. As she watched, she saw Will enter the house. Jay removed the shooter' pistol, rolled him over onto his prone position and made her way down the bank to check out the shooter's car. As she suspected there was nothing in the car. As she reached her own car, out of the corner of her eye, she saw Will sprint across the road. She was very surprised and she could only assume that Will was going to look for the shooter. She smiled to herself. *Brave but foolish*, she thought. Fortunately she had killed the shooter as Will would certainly be no match for him. Jay saw an opportunity, if Will was not in the house, this gave Jay a chance to search. She crossed the road and headed down the side of the house, undercover so Will would not be able to see her from the bank. She entered the house via the back door and headed straight into Toby McCloud's study where she thought would be the best place to start looking. She first pulled all the books off the shelves and flicked through the leaves making sure there was nothing hidden in them. She then started on the desk pulling out the drawers and checking in the cavities to make sure there was nothing hidden in the gaps. She was aware of the passing time but was surprised when she heard a voice call out, 'I know you are in there I am armed and am coming in.' Jay didn't want Will to see her. She had already spotted the window and had opened it for a quick getaway if necessary. She climbed out and in a crouching run raced for the cover of the trees in the near distance. She didn't expect Will to shoot and she made cover without any incident. She made her way back to her car and headed back to Glasgow feeling that Will was safe again for the time being.

Chapter Forty-Two

'Wow,' said Will, 'that's twice you have saved my life, to say nothing of the help on the "Bruno".'

'All in a day's work,' replied Jay, still lying in bed.

'So when did you start following me?' asked Will.

'When we heard that Toby McCloud wanted to show you something, the team believed that the house of cards might be about to tumble. We assumed that the oppo had also tapped your phone and knew you were going to learn something from McCloud. We thought that you were in danger so Allan and Brown flew up on the same flight as you and followed you up to McCloud's house.

'Now, finally, tell me about Sam's house?' asked Will.

'Via our tap, we heard you were going to see Sam. We had also been watching and tapping Sljonic and when we heard that he was going to pay Sam a visit too, we mobilised as we knew there would be trouble and you in the middle,' replied Jay.

'How did I get shot and injured?' asked Will. 'The last thing I remember was you pointing a gun at me and firing!'

'As you will recall, it was chaos with everyone firing at everyone. It was my job to protect you. As I looked around the room, I saw you just standing fixed to the spot and behind you one of Sljonic's men was pointing a gun at you. I fired at him and as he fired you dived to you left. He was dead but I thought you were, too. I could see that you had been shot but the serious issue was your head wound from the table that you hit when you dived. The rest is history. We caught Sljonic alive but his two accomplices were killed.'

Will thought for a moment.

'What about the fourth one?' asked Will.

'What fourth one? There were only three!'

'No, there were definitely four. Sljonic and his two heavies but there was also the one who broke the door down with one of those barrel type hammers but he didn't come in with the other three. If you didn't get him, he must have got away.'

Jay picked up her phone from the bedside table and relayed the new information back to a nameless voice at the other end.

'What everyone wants is that sheet of paper with what I now know are bank account passwords but there is one letter missing from the end of each password. No one so far, including Crombie, knows what those letters are, therefore, we are not at the top of the tree. There is someone else out there who has the code and therefore is the man behind this whole operation.'

'Or a woman,' retorted Jay, 'we mustn't be sexist in our approach to master criminals and terrorists, I think I have done as much killing as the next man in this operation,' said Jay.

'Whatever, but seriously, whilst that person is out there I am still at risk,' replied Will.

'The difference now is that you have your own personal bodyguard,' retorted Jay. 'But what about Sam, you haven't told me what he said when you confronted him with impersonating you?' asked Jay.

'He denied knowing much about who was organising the operation, although I think he had suspicions and was going to give me a name when the gangsters, or whoever they were, arrived and that all ended with Sam being killed as you know.'

'Very convenient, if you ask me,' replied Jay.

'Yes, I was thinking that, too. Same as Toby. Any possible break in the chain and they are dealt with. What does Allan think you are doing? Does he know you are with me?'

'No, I don't think so. He believes that we are irreversible enemies. I said I wanted some time off to be with my daughter.'

'OK, does he think there is someone else in this operation?'

'Definitely, he doesn't believe Crombie has the brains to run this operation, so his instructions are the same as before, wait and watch.'

'You mean while I get killed in the process,' replied Will.

'I think Allan is quite impressed with your survival instincts and that you are in no more risk than you have ever been. However, I believe he will be watching you. There was no one outside last night when I arrived. I did a circuit of the block before I knocked. Though, when I leave I think I should go via the gate at the bottom of your garden and into the lane at the back.'

'OK, but who is the ringleader, it must be somebody that knows me and the firm to have enlisted Sam and Crombie. Someone with money and influence,' Will paused, 'my god, I think I know who it is and I think I know what the code is.'

'Who, what, tell me.'

Will told her.

'That makes some sense,' she replied.

'Fancy a trip to the Virgin Islands for a spot of business?' asked Will.

'Shall I pack my bikini, too?'

'Sounds like a good idea,' replied Will.

Will booked a hotel and arranged some flights on the Internet.

'I have booked us on the 10.20 flight tomorrow morning. There are no direct flights to the Virgin Islands so we are going via Antigua. To save an early morning start, I have booked us into a hotel at Gatwick for the night.'

'All sounds good to me,' replied Jay.

Will agreed to pick Jay from her house later in the day. Jay left by the back gate.

Chapter Forty-Three

As the cab pulled out from in front of Will's house to pick up Jay, Will turned to check the house looked occupied with the normal security lights on, and as he did so, he noticed another car pull out behind the cab. He watched it surreptitiously for a while and it seemed to be following the cab. He called Jay.

'I think I may have a tail. I can't pick you up at your house.'

Jay thought for a moment.

'Get the driver to drop you outside Tesco's in the High Street, pay him to wait outside for ten minutes, the tail will think you will be coming back, walk straight through the store and I will pick you up in a cab from the car park behind.'

As the cab approached the Tesco store, Will told the cab driver that he had changed his mind and if he could stop outside Tesco but he must wait ten minutes before driving off. Will slipped the fare and a large tip onto the seat next to the driver.

'Remember, ten minutes, please.'

'OK, mate and thanks for the large tip,' came the reply.

Will walked briskly into the store, skirted down a few isles, in case he had been followed and out the rear door into the car park. He spotted Jay's taxi almost immediately and hopped in with his rucksack.

As Jay's cab came of out the supermarket's car park, both Jay and Will slid down in their seats, so any tail still there would not see them.

The following morning, as they sat in the departure lounge to catch their flight to firstly St. John's on Antigua and then onward to Tortola in the British Virgin Islands, Will hoped that they were going to find the next part of the puzzle.

Chapter Forty-Four

The flight was not busy and Will had booked BA Club World seats and although it was before noon, they soon settled down in their seats sipping champagne. When they were up in the air, Jay did some research on the British Virgin Islands. She read to Will, extracts from her tablet.

'Apparently, The Virgin Islands were first settled by the Arawak from South America around 100 BC. The Arawaks inhabited the islands until the 15th century when they were displaced by the more aggressive Caribs, a tribe from the Lesser Antilles Islands, after whom the Caribbean Sea is named.

'The first European sighting of the Virgin Islands was by Christopher Columbus in 1493 on his second voyage to the Americas. Columbus gave them the fanciful name *Santa Ursula y las Once Mil Vírgenes* (Saint Ursula and her Eleven Thousand Virgins), shortened to *Las Vírgenes* (The Virgins).

'The Spanish claimed the islands by discovery in the early 16th century, but never settled them, and subsequent years saw the English, Dutch, French, Spanish, and Danish all jostling for control of the region, which became a notorious haunt for pirates. There is no record of any native Amerindian population in the British Virgin Islands during this period, although the native population on nearby Saint Croix was decimated.

'The Dutch established a settlement on the island of Tortola by 1648. In 1672, the English captured Tortola from the Dutch. The official name of the British territory is the Virgin Islands, and the official name of the U.S. territory is the Virgin Islands of the United States. In practice, the two island groups are almost universally referred to as the British Virgin Islands and the U.S. Virgin Islands.'

'Umm,' replied Will.

'There is more,' said Jay as she continued to read from her tablet. 'The original inhabitants of the Islands are thought to have perished during the colonial period due to enslavement, foreign disease, and mass extermination brought about by European colonists as is the case in the rest of the Caribbean.

'European colonists later settled here and established sugar plantations, at least one tobacco plantation, and purchased slaves acquired from Africa. The plantations are gone, but the descendants of the slaves remain the bulk of the population, sharing a common African-Caribbean heritage with the rest of the English-speaking Caribbean.

'In 1916 and 1917, Denmark and the U.S., respectively, ratified a treaty, in which Denmark sold the Danish West Indies to the United States of America for $25 million in gold.'

'What a fountain of knowledge you are. Does the information tell us the best places to eat?' enquired Will, as he sipped more champagne.

'You are a heathen, Will Slater, typical lawyer,' came the reply back from Jay. 'Anyway, I haven't finished yet.

'The 150-square-kilometre (58-square-mile) British Virgin Islands consist of the main islands of Tortola, Virgin Gorda, Anegada, and Jost Van Dyke, along with over fifty other smaller islands and cays. About fifteen of the islands are inhabited. The capital, Road Town, is situated on Tortola, the largest island, which is about 20 km long and 5 km wide. The islands had a population of about 28,000.

'Financial services account for over half of the income of the territory. The majority of this revenue is generated by the licensing of offshore companies and related services. The British Virgin Islands is a significant global player in the offshore financial services industry. In 2000, it was reported in a survey of offshore jurisdictions for the United Kingdom government that over 45% of the world's offshore companies were formed in the British Virgin Islands. However, since 2001, financial services in the British Virgin Islands have been regulated by the Independent Financial Services Commission.'

Jay was interrupted.

'Would you like wine with your meal, madam?' asked the hostess.

Jay peered at the menu card that had been place on the table in front of her, 'Yes, please red, the Shiraz, please.'

'You, sir?'

'Same please.'

'That's a relief, I didn't think I could take much more of the history of the BVIs, as us heathen lawyers call them,' said Will winking at Jay.

'What I don't understand,' said Jay, 'is why they opened bank accounts here as it is no longer a tax haven. I remember David Cameron, when he was Prime Minister, making this point and citing other areas in the world which were tax havens.'

'Well, this is not about hiding tax. This is about security and the availability of the funds when they are needed. Everyone knows where Java PLC is registered and its only director is me. As far as I can recall from the company's accounts, the full amount of tax had been accounted for and I assume paid at the appropriate time. When you come to think of it, the one thing you don't want is the authorities snooping around for undeclared tax when the purpose of the company is to hide something much bigger.'

After a leisurely lunch they both decided that they would skip the films and catch up on some sleep for the rest of the eight-hour flight.

They were woken, 45 minutes before landing, and by the time they had had a stretch and freshened up, the seat belt signs were on as the plane made its approach into VC Bird International Airport in St. John's.

They had travelled light with only hand luggage, so as soon as they disembarked they made their way over to the Air Sunshine desk to book flights to Road Town airport on Tortola.

'When is the next available flight to Road Town please?' asked Will to the desk receptionist.

'How many travelling, sir?' she asked.

'Just the two of us,' replied Will turning and indicating Jay and himself.

'You are in luck, sir,' said the receptionist in the evocative sign song voice, typical of West Indians', the next flight is in 30 minutes and we have two seats available.'

'Fantastic, thank you. How long is the flight?'

'About an hour, sir, depending on how good the pilot is in landing,' and burst into laughter, 'only joking, all our pilots are excellent.'

Will paid on his credit card and they made their way to the departure gate to catch their flight.

When they were up in the air, Jay pulled out her tablet again.

'It says here Road Town, located on Tortola, is the capital of the British Virgin Islands. It is situated on the horseshoe-shaped Road Harbour in the centre of the island's south coast. The population was about 9,400 in 2004.The name is derived from the nautical term "the roads", a place less sheltered than a harbour but which ships can easily get to. A 28 hectares (69 acres) development called Wickham's Cay, consisting of two areas that were reclaimed from the sea and a marina, have enabled Road Town to emerge as a haven for yacht chartering and a centre of tourism. This area is the newest part of the city and the hub for the new commercial and administrative buildings of the BVI. The oldest building in Road Town, HM Prison on Main Street, was built in 1774.'

'Well, we don't want to be paying any visits there, thanks,' replied Will.

'We will be flying into Terrence B. Lettsome International Airport.'

'Not very international as there are no flights from anywhere else other than local hops and who is Terrence B. Lettsome?' asked Will.

'Ah,' replied Jay, once again tapping on her tablet. 'So you are interested in my research. Do you want the short or long version?'

'Shortest possible please, as I am now in travel guide overload,' laughed Will.

'OK, Terrance Buckley Lettsome died in 2007 age 72 and was a politician after whom the main airport in the British Virgin Islands is named. He was one of the Territory's longest-serving legislators and retired in 1999 after 36 years of uninterrupted service. So, there we go. Named after him in his honour.'

The Captain informed his passengers by intercom that the time in Road Town was 4.30 in the afternoon. Will looked at his watch, 8.30 p.m. in London.

At the airport, they got a cab to the hotel Will had booked them into, "Sebastian's on the Beach". Will had read the good comments on Trip Advisor and it was, as the name said, right on the beach.

They checked into the hotel and decided on a swim before dinner. There was a small beach attached to the hotel and the water was wonderfully warm with that typical turquoise-coloured sea of the Caribbean.

After their swim, they showered and headed down for a pre-dinner drink. They sat under green sun umbrellas overlooking the beach with palm trees gently swaying in the warm breeze with a backcloth of the sea and a pallet of colours from greens, blues and greys. Will sipped his gin and tonic and, for a moment, forgot the reason why they were there and the fact he was still under the suspicion of multiple murders and running a company for the benefit of terrorism.

After a dinner of Caribbean lobster and Chardonnay and a final drink on the terrace, the travelling and the time difference finally got the better of them and they both collapsed into bed for a deep dreamless sleep.

In the morning Will phoned the bank.

'Tortola Private Bank, good morning,' came the voice over the phone.

'Good morning, can I speak to Mr Justerini, please?' asked Will.

'May I ask who is calling?'

'Will Slater.'

'Just a moment, please, I am putting you through.'

After a brief gap a voice answered.

'Mr Slater, how good to hear from you again so soon. How can I help?'

'Mr Justerini, I am in Road Town and wondered if I could pop in for a meeting to discuss my banking arrangements.'

After a slight pause, 'Of course, Mr Slater, I hope you have brought all the proper access information with you, otherwise, I won't be able to discuss anything very much.'

'No problem, Mr Justerini, I think I have everything. What time would suit you?'

'Shall we say 12 noon at my office?'

'Perfect, see you later, Mr Justerini,' replied Will.

Will and Jay had a couple of hours before the meeting, so they decided to do some sightseeing. They walked to the pier and then to the centre of town. After the placid tropical exterior of the Victorian style government buildings, the centre of town had a much more business feel about it, even amongst the bars, shops and the market. They stopped outside the Tortala Private Bank and Will agreed to meet Jay in about an hour for lunch. They kissed goodbye and Will walked into the bank and into the marble banking hall which had the feel of few decades past.

'Mr Justerini, please,' asked Will.

'Certainly, sir, your name, please?'

'Will Slater.'

The receptionist picked up his phone and announced Will's arrival.

'Mr Justerini will be with you in a moment, sir. Please take a seat over there,' indicating some comfy looking settees in the corner of the banking hall.

Before long an elegant, be-suited man, walked across to Will.

'Mr Slater? Dominic Justerini,' he said offering his hand in greeting.

'Good afternoon, Mr Justerini, thank you for seeing me at such short notice.'

Justerini lead Will into his private office and with a sweeping gesture indicated for Will to sit down on the opposite side of his desk.

'Now, how can I help you, Mr Slater?' asked Justerini.

'I would like to transfer all my funds to a different account, please. These are the details of the new account,' said Will passing a sheet of paper across to the bank manager.

'I am sorry that you are ceasing to use this bank, I hope we have done nothing to cause any issues?'

'No, not at all I just need to have the funds more readily available,' replied Will.

'I understand,' said Justerini in a resigned way. 'Can I have all the details, please? First the five long numbers.'

Will took another sheet of paper from his jacket pocket and slid it over the Banker's highly polished desk.

Justerini spent the next minute typing details into his computer.

'Now, the five key letters, please.'

Will reached across for a pad and pen on the Banker's desk and wrote down the five letters and passed the pad across to Justerini.

Justerini looked at them and keyed the letters into the computer.

Will waited in some concern, hoping that he had guessed correctly the five letters.

'That all looks correct. Thank you, Mr Slater. The banks on the Island do not operate during the middle of the day so I will attend to this transfer when I return after lunch.'

'OK. Could I ask you for a copy of the instructions, please?' asked Will.

'Well, I suppose so,' said Justerini looking slightly annoyed.

Justerini typed again and then pressed a key with a flourish and got up and walked across his office to a printer in the corner which was churning out the requested piece of paper.

'Could you just sign it and print your name on the bottom please, Mr Justerini?' asked Will. 'Not all banks are as efficient as yours and I would like a record in case there are any issues later on.'

'I suppose so but it is a little unusual,' replied Justerini.

He signed the paper and passed it across to Will.

The banker then got up indicating that as far as he was concerned the meeting was over.

Will got up too and shook the banker's hand.

'Thank you for your time and for dealing with my money over the years, Mr Justerini. I hope we can do business again in the future.'

'I hope so, too,' replied the banker with little enthusiasm.

Will left the bank. But he didn't go far. He walked across the road and waited under the shade of a palm tree opposite the front door of the bank.

As soon as Will had left his office, Justerini unlocked the top drawer in his desk and removed the piece of paper with the two telephone numbers. He dialled the first number. The phone was picked up but no reply.

'Slater has been into the bank with all the correct passwords and has asked to transfer all the funds,' Justerini said down the receiver.

'Thank you for letting me know. No doubt you will hold up the transfer until we can make other arrangements for Mr Slater,' came the reply down the phone.

'I will make myself scarce for the rest of the day in case he checks that the transfer has not taken place,' replied the banker.

'Thank you Justerini. I will transfer $100,000 in your personal account immediately for the service provided.'

Justerini hardly had time to say thank you when the line went dead.

Justerini then dialled the second number on the paper.

The phone went immediately to automated voicemail. Justerini delivered the same message and then disconnected.

Justerini locked the piece of paper back in his desk drawer and made a third call.

'Hello, darling, I have had rather a good morning and wondered if you fancy an expensive lunch and an afternoon at the flat relaxing?'

The recipient of the call replied in the affirmative.

Justerini put on his jacket and left the bank with a jaunty and satisfied air.

Chapter Forty-Five

From his spot in the shade Will watched Justerini leave the bank heading off down the road. Will crossed the street and entered the bank again. He walked up to the banking desk and asked if one of the tellers could help him.

'I will try, sir, what can I do?'

'I need to make some transfers that have been authorised by Mr Justerini,' said Will slipping the signed sheet across the counter, 'but he said he was rather busy and rushing to a meeting so I thought I might ask if you could do it for me?'

'Well, Mr Justerini deals with all these sorts of transactions. Let me phone him.' The teller picked up the phone and dialled a number.

Will knew there would be no reply. The danger was that the teller would try Justerini's mobile.

'He does appear to be out and he doesn't like anyone phoning him on his mobile during lunch in case he is with an important client,' replied the teller. 'Ummm, it all seems to be authorised and correctly signed so I don't suppose it will matter if I do it for him.'

'I thought all the banks had a siesta at lunchtime?' asked Will.

The teller looked at Will in an old-fashioned way.

'We are in the modern age, Mr Slater, 24/7' was the reply.

The teller then spent a couple of minutes tapping on his keyboard.

'There you are, Mr Slater, all done. Can you access your account from your phone and check the money has been received?'

Will took out his phone, opened an app and keyed in the password and waited.

'Yes, all there. Thank you very much for attending to that for me.'

'A pleasure, Mr Slater, have a good day now.'

Will left the bank for the second time and headed off to meet Jay.

They had agreed to meet at one of the guidebook's recommended restaurants, Pusser's Road Town Pub. With a view over the pier, they tried the local cocktail called a painkiller, made up of dark rum, cream of coconut and pineapple and orange juices. The cocktails accompanied a lunch of seafood chowder, curried chicken, and jerk pork roti, an island-style wrap made with flatbread, served with mango chutney.

After lunch they sauntered back to their hotel where they decided an hour in bed before a swim would be a perfect end to the afternoon.

Chapter Forty-Six

Justerini's good mood had not diminished when he arrived back at the Bank, a little before 5 p.m. having had a very fine lobster lunch with a very expensive bottle of Chablis, followed by an afternoon romping with his mistress in a flat that he had bought her overlooking the beach.

As the banker sauntered back to his private office, the Teller who had dealt with Will called across the banking hall.

'I have dealt with the transfers for Mr Slater as you authorised, Mr Justerini,' said the teller looking pleased with himself.

Justerini stopped in his tracks and suddenly felt very sick. He walked over to the teller.

'I am sorry, what did you say?' asked Justerini hoping that he had misheard the teller.

'I dealt with Mr Slater's transfers as per your authority.' Seeing Justerini's face the teller added, 'I hope that was OK?'

Justerini was speechless. He would normally have dealt with any breaching of his procedures very strongly but in truth the teller had done nothing wrong and if he criticised the teller, Justerini would need to explain why the transfer was incorrect. So, he just turned around and walked with slumped shoulders back to his office. He sat down heavily into his expensive desk chair and once again unlocked his drawer and removed the piece of paper with the two telephone numbers.

He dialled the first number. The call was picked up the other end.

'There has been a terrible mistake. One of my staff made the transfers for Slater without asking me,' Justerini said down the receiver.

'That is really bad news for us all including you, Mr Justerini,' came the reply.

'I will, of course, repay the $100,000 immediately,' Justerini said in a winey voice.

'I fear that will not be enough recompense for such a grave error, Mr Justerini.' The line went dead.

Justerini sat in his chair for a few moments with the phone in his hand pondering what recompense he was likely to have to make.

He put down the receiver and dialled the second number. Once again, the number went straight to automated voicemail and Justerini repeated the same message. Suddenly, such a good day had turned into a nightmare because of a stupid error. Tears trickled down his cheeks and made splodges on his desk blotter.

Chapter Forty-Seven

Will and Jay flew back to London the next day. On the journey home, Will explained to Jay how he expected events to unfold once they were back in London. At Heathrow, they took separate taxis. Jay went home to pick up some more clothes and agreed that she would come straight back via the back gate route.

Will took his taxi straight home. He didn't notice anyone watching outside but he was not worried as he was expecting a visitor fairly soon.

Will took his bag upstairs and unpacked.

He then made a telephone call. The conversation was short.

Jay arrived via the back gate in the garden and both sat in the kitchen and waited.

'How long do you think we will have to wait?' asked Jay.

'Not long. Although I didn't see anyone watching the house, I suspect someone will have seen my return.' Will looked at his watch. 'I have been back here ninety minutes, so I estimate quite soon.'

They both sat back in their chairs across the kitchen table from each other, drank a cup of coffee, as the clock ticked.

After fifteen minutes the front door bell rang. Will looked across to Jay and raised his eyebrows, got up and walked to the front door.

'Hello, Will,' the visitor said as Will opened the front door.

'Hello, Michael, I have been expecting you, why don't you come in?'

In stepped Michael Bore.

'When did you work it out?' asked Michael.

'About three days ago.'

'Are you alone?' asked Michael as he walked towards the kitchen door. 'Haven't got that gun-totting Annie Oakley here then?'

'No, I am alone,' lied Will.

Michael stepped through into the kitchen and looked around. He noticed just one cup on the table.

'Let's go onto the lounge. Would you like a drink?' asked Will

'OK,' replied Michael.

'What would you like, whisky?' asked Will, as Michael settled himself down onto one of the settees.

'That's fine thank you.'

Will poured two glasses of whisky, gave one to Michael and sat in the opposite settee.

'Cheers,' Will said, looking very relaxed.

'OK, Will, let's cut all the crap. I want my money back. I think we can come to an arrangement where you can walk away into the sunset and be forgotten.'

'Sorry, Michael, I don't understand, what money?'

'Don't be stupid, Will. I know you have been to the Virgin Islands and know you have transferred all my money to your account.'

'Michael, if it is your money, how could I have transferred it? As far as I recall, all the accounts were in the name of Java, with one director, who was me. Could this have been your one mistake in this sordid scam that you involved me in? Which, also, nearly got me killed on a number of occasions. Seems like fair recompense to me,' said Will as he smiled annoyingly at Michael.

'Don't be clever with me, Will. This is a dangerous game that you're playing and it won't end up well for you. Just let me have the money and we will all forget this has happened.'

'I don't think that will work, Michael, as I am now so closely linked to a number of murders. I need answers to enable me to clear my name. Humour me, Michael, explain how this all works,' said Will.

'It is all very simple or was until you took matters into your own hands. I warned you at the office to be careful,' Bore continued, 'Crombie used his connections throughout the world to source used and decommissioned weapons from previous

169

war zones and to sell them to terrorist groups. Crombie did this through an Eastern European company which repaired and shipped the weapons. Crombie had a share there, too, I think but most of his money came from the sales, which he organised.'

'Yes, Sljovic Inc., were the suppliers I have come across them, too! But why involve you Michael, he seems to have all areas covered and you are a respected businessman and surely you don't need the proceeds from crime?' asked Will.

'I was in trouble, overstretched and going bankrupt. A couple of my businesses were failing and I needed some quick cash to keep them going and maintain my lifestyle. Someone found out and Crombie approached me. At first, I thought perhaps you had put him up to it but then realised that was not your style. It had to have been someone else in your office who had spotted my difficulties. Anyway, Crombie offered me a way out of the problem. He told me that I was going to be the middle man with the Eastern Europeans and he didn't exist as far as they were concerned.'

'So you were behind Toby's and Foundling's deaths?' asked Will.

'No, I had nothing to do with that, it was Crombie who decided that they had to be got rid of,' replied Bore.

'Well, who killed them and why?' asked Will.

'I imagine Sljovic's mob, under Crombie's instructions, but who knows why and as far as I am concerned who cares,' said Bore asserting his position again.

'So did you send the pirates?' asked Will.

'Bloody well didn't. Cost me over two grand to replace that tender you cut loose. I have always told you that the sea is a dangerous place,' laughed Bore. 'Anyway, I have had enough of humouring you, I want the money.'

There was a creak of a floorboard in the hall. Michael was up in a flash, pulling out a pistol from his coat pocket and pointed it at Will's head.

'Come in, whoever you are or I will shoot him,' called out Bore.

In stepped Jay.

'Ah Annie Oakley herself. You are probably too young to know who that is so let's call you,' Bore paused, 'I know, Lara

170

Croft. Step forward and put your hands in the air,' commanded Bore.

Bore took a step towards Will and pressed the barrel of his gun against Will's temple.

'Now, you wouldn't want me to make a mess of lover boy's head, would you? I know you will be armed so slowly using your left hand remove your gun and throw it on the floor.'

Jay slowly reached behind her and using her left hand plucked her pistol from the waistband of her trousers and lobbed it into the middle of the room.

'Good girl, now come and sit down on the settee here,' said Bore indicating with his left hand.

'You sit down next to her,' Bore said to Will.

Bore then kicked Jay's gun out of both their reaches and while keeping his eye on them, bent down and picked it up. He put it into the pocket of his coat.

'Well, now, what am I going to do with you two? I could shoot you both but I won't get my money. So, I have a plan. Get up, darling and come over here,' said Bore indicating to Jay, 'kneel down facing your mate.'

Jay knelt down and Bore put his gun to her head.

'Now, Will my money for the life of your girl here.'

Chapter Forty-Eight

Jay heard Michael enter the hall and ask whether he was alone, in that split second she picked up her cup and slipped into the utility room, keeping the door ajar so she could hear any conversation. He heard Bore and Will come into the kitchen and then leave to go into the lounge. Jay pulled out her phone and made a quick call. She took off her shoulder holster and placed the gun in her waistband. She then left the utility room made her way through the kitchen towards the lounge.

She could hear Will and Bore talking but as she didn't know the house well, she stepped on a creaking floorboard and heard Bore call out, 'Come in here whoever you are or I will shoot him.'

Jay stepped into the lounge.

Chapter Forty-Nine

Jay felt the pressure of the gun against the back of her head.

'Don't say anything, Will,' called out Jay.

'Shut up you, bitch. If I don't get my money, I will surely kill you both. Last chance Will. I have got nothing to lose.'

'OK, Michael you win. The details are in my study.'

'Whereabouts?'

'On my desk, in a folder marked Virgin Islands,' replied Will.

'OK, this is how we are going to do this. You go first, Will and then you, bitch and if either of you make a false move, I will shoot.'

Will got up and walked towards the door. Bore backed away and indicated that Jay should get up and walk behind Will towards the study. The three of them in a line with Bore keeping the gun close to Jay's head.

As Bore passed through the lounge door another gun appeared close to his head.

'I think I will have that gun, please, Mr Bore,' a voice said from just outside the doorway.

Bore turned slightly and saw SO 15 agent, Harry Allan standing in the hall pointing his gun at his head.

'I will take that, Michael,' said Jay as she removed the pistol from Bore's hand.

'I think the game is up, Michael,' said Allan. 'You are going to spend a long time in prison.'

'You are going to have to prove I have any involvement in whatever you think I have done,' replied Bore.

Will glared across at Bore.

'I don't think we will have much difficulty,' said Allan.

Just then the front door crashed open.

'Armed police, do not move, put your guns down, on your knees, hands in the air,' shouted a voice from a burly policeman, dressed in dark blue with a Kevlar vest and a vicious looking weapon pointing at everyone.

'Don't move, down on your knees,' the policeman shouted again as seven more policeman rushed through the front door. One covering the four kneeling in the hall, three searching the downstairs and four rushing up the stairs.

As Will knelt, he wondered if any of this armed response team were the ones who attended the last visit. He wanted to shout out, 'If you need to use the bathroom, you know where it is,' but thought better of it.

'All clear downstairs,' came a voice from the kitchen.

'All clear upstairs,' came another policeman's voice.

The policeman in the hall without taking his eyes off the four on the floor, turned his head slightly and called out in the direction of the front door. 'All clear.'

For a moment everything seemed to have stopped and strangely the only noise was a chirrup from the phone in Bore's pocket as a new message came through.

Then in walked Inspector Dawkin with Sergeant Edgar in tow.

Dawkin, also wearing a Kevlar vest which made him look like some exotic bird with its chest all puffed out, circled and walked between the kneeling supplicants as if they were exhibits at an exhibition.

'Well, well, well, we have got all the players in this little extravaganza all together. Good job, eh, Edgar?'

'Yes, Gov, good job,' replied Edgar.

Allan piped up. 'We are both SO15,' he said indicating with his head towards Jay, 'you have got to let us go.'

Dawkin turned towards Allan, 'I don't know who you are but would be pleased if you would shut up or one of my men will shoot you. Do you understand?'

Allan nodded.

'Right, cuff them and give them their rights and get them down to Paddington pronto. I am really going to enjoy this,' said Dawkin chuckling to himself as he left the house.

Chapter Fifty

There was a knock on Justerini's door and his secretary entered and said,

'There are three gentlemen to see you, sir.'

'Did they say where they were from?' Justerini asked.

'No, sir, but they look official.'

'OK, you had better show them in.'

Justerini stood as three men entered his office.

'Good morning, Mr Justerini, my name is Chris Melody and I am from the Financial Services Commission and these two gentlemen are from the police.'

'How might I help you?' asked the banker.

'We have reason to believe that you have broken client confidentially and, also, taken fees personally for transactions made through the bank.'

'Absolutely ridiculous. What proof do you have?'

'Actually, quite a lot sir, thanks to a whistle blower, including information on your personal account which seems to have quite a considerable balance considering the size of your salary, including a transfer into it, only two days ago, for $100,000. We understand from a lady, who asked to be nameless, that you own an expensive beachside apartment. Apparently, your wife knows nothing about this property?'

'You haven't spoken to my wife, have you? How dare you. This has nothing to do with her!' shouted Justerini.

'Normally, we wouldn't immediately, but the whistle blower lead us to believe that we should speak to her first. As it turned out, this was a false lead, but she was quite shocked about the apartment.'

Justerini slumped into his chair. This was the recompense that had been promised over the phone. Ruin and probably jail.

'Therefore, we have no alternative but to arrest you on these charges, Mr Justerini,' responded Melody. 'Please, come with us.'

The two policemen walked around to the other side of the desk, maneuvered the banker onto his feet, walked him out through the banking hall and into their police car.

Chapter Fifty-One

Will immediately recognised the police station, as Paddington Green, situated just off Edgware Road in central West London.

Paddington Green Police Station serves as the most important high-security station in the United Kingdom. This is because prisoners suspected of terrorism are held at the station for questioning. The building was built in the 1960s, and underneath the station are sixteen cells located below ground level, which have a separate custody suite from the building's other cells. High-profile terrorist suspects arrested across the UK are often taken to Paddington Green Police Station for interrogation, and held until escorted to a court of law. Suspects who have been held there include members of the IRA, the British nationals released from Guantanamo Bay, and the 21 July 2005 London bombers.

After being searched and having his belt and all valuables taken away, Will was lead to his cell, and although supposed to be more luxurious than a normal police cell, which only have a toilet and a mattress, was not a place where he wanted to spend too long. The cell was lined with brown paper, which he found out later, was so that any traces of explosives found on suspect bodies can be proven not to have been picked up from the cells. Will knew from his law knowledge that suspects could be kept up to twenty-eight days without charge. He certainly hoped that this would not be the case with him. However, he sat on the bed with the belief that his stay would not be that short. After nearly two hours, he heard his cell door lock being released and two guards informed him he was going for interrogation.

Will was handcuffed again and lead to an interview room. They were still below ground level and although the room was well lit, its sparseness sent a shiver up Will's spine.

Will sat down at a table facing Dawkin and another man. At the corner of the desk, stood a black recording machine.

'Mr Slater, this is Chief Inspector Kinsey of the Anti-Terrorist Division of the Met Police and he has kindly let me attend this interview with you, as we have past history,' said Dawkin with a smug look on his face.

'I should have my solicitor present before I answer any questions,' said Will.

'I hope that won't be necessary, Mr Slater,' interjected Kinsey, in a deep booming voice. 'We are not going to charge you, in fact, we are about to release you as we are satisfied that you were innocent in this matter which has been confirmed by SO 15 and indeed the initial testimony given by Mr Bore.'

'You mean Bore has admitted to everything and exonerated me?' asked Will.

'Yes, he has said that he was behind the whole scheme,' replied Kinsey.

'And the murders? Are you satisfied that I had nothing to do with those?' asked Will.

'Well, that is more Inspector Dawkin's case than mine,' said Kinsey looking across to Dawkin, 'and although there are a few loose ends we are pretty satisfied that Bore and his associates were responsible for those too.'

Dawkin nodded although Will thought he didn't look entirely sure and rather disappointed.

'You will have to appear as a witness when it goes to court but for now you are free to go Mr Slater.' Kinsey and Dawkin got up. An officer will show you the way out.

Just as Dawkin was leaving the interview room he turned and said, 'Thank you for the call Slater, but in my mind the case remains open as there are too many unanswered questions but there appears not to be enough evidence to hold you further.'

Will sat at the table for a moment taking in what had been said to him. But then realised that he wanted to get out before anyone changed their mind. The officer showed him up to the main entrance hall of the police station, which functioned as any normal police station. Waiting in a chair in the corner was Jay. When she saw Will, she rushed up and hugged him.

'Let's get home,' he said.

Chapter Fifty-Two

Mellnic had watched the offices of Slater & Craig from his vantage point in the café across the road for several days, watching for patterns and trying to establish who was George Wright. He had told the café owner that he was a private detective and was watching for an illicit liaison. If asked, the café owner would recognise Mellnic anyway, so telling him any story would probably make no difference. In any case, he was not planning on frequenting this café again, particularly as the coffee and food were not very good. It was not that easy spotting a pattern as there were other companies in the same building. But a pattern was emerging. Slater & Craig worked much longer hours than the other companies. Mellnic could tell this by when the lights were switched off on each floor. He established that the later employees leaving were from the solicitors' office. So, on the fourth evening, he particularly concentrated on people leaving after 6 p.m. when the lights on the other floors had gone out. Fortunately, the front of the office block was well lit and he could quite clearly see everyone leaving the building. 7 p.m. came and went and, as usual, the café owner reminded Mellnic that he would be closing at 8pm. The lights started going out on the third floor and at about 7.45, a large man exited the front doors, looked left and right and strode off in the direction of the tube. Mellnic was sure that this was George Wright from his picture on the firm's web site. He hurriedly left a twenty-pound note on the table, probably more than was owed and certainly more than the value but he didn't want any conversation with the owner who was hovering to shut up shop; and exited the café in pursuit of Wright. Wright didn't head down into the tube but hailed a taxi around the corner. Mellnic looked around but there were no other empty taxis available, so he had lost his target.

He couldn't bear the thought of another coffee laden day in that crummy café. He then had an idea. He had noticed a small shop that sold cards and stationary close to the station and perhaps it would still be open. With luck it was, but it looked as if it was just closing. He bought a large brown envelope and a small notebook. He then took a copy of the free Evening Standard paper from the stand in front of the station and stuffed it into the envelope and sealed it. From the website details on his phone, he wrote in capital letters George Wright's full name, the name and address of the firm and wrote URGENT in large letters across the top. He then walked back to the Slater & Craig offices. He could see there were still lights on the third floor.

He strode across to the reception desk.

'Urgent delivery for Slater & Craig,' said Mellnic to the receptionist, for a moment wondering whether his Eastern European accent was going to be an issue but then realised that many of the deliveries were now undertaken by individuals from his former part of the world.

'OK, leave it with me and I will take it up,' replied the receptionist.

'Can't do that, it has to be delivered in person to George Wright.'

The receptionist tutted, and picked up the phone and spoke to someone, who Mellnic assumed was in the Slater & Craig office.

'OK, third floor and someone will meet you at the lift,' said the receptionist.

Mellnic took the lift to the third floor and sure enough as the door opened a very attractive woman was standing there smiling.

'Good evening, I gather you have a package for Slater & Craig,' she said.

'Yes, I do, it is urgent and has to be delivered personally to George Wright, one of your partners,' added Mellnic to show that he had some knowledge of the firm which he hoped would add more creditability.

'Leave it with me and I will let George have it in the morning, he has gone for the night.'

'Well, I am supposed to deliver it in person. I was told not to give it to anyone else and to get it signed for. I don't think I can leave it with you.' Mellnic half turned away and as if having a second thought turned back.

'Could I deliver it to his home? I would feel better if I could, as I understand it is very urgent.'

'Well, I am afraid we don't give out home addresses of either the partners or the staff.' Seeing that Mellnic remained unmoved by that comment and wanting to get home herself she said, 'Wait here and I will ring George and see if he wants you to deliver it to his home or not.' With that she swept back into the main reception area of the solicitors' office flicking down the catch so Mellnic could not follow her in.

After a couple of minutes she returned with a piece of paper.

'George doesn't know what the papers are that you have, but he is working on a number of deals, so he says it is OK for you to deliver the package to his home. I have written the address on this piece of paper,' said the woman handing it over to Mellnic.

'OK, thanks a lot,' said Mellnic looking down at the address, 'I will get along there now.'

Mellnic retraced his steps back into the street and looked up George's address on the map on his phone.

Mellnic found George Wright's address was in a very smart part of London, in Knightsbridge. The front of the property faced the side entrance of Harrods, the iconic department store. Mellnic walked up the half dozen steps to the main door and studied the names by the side of each bell and pressed one.

'Package for Wright,' said Mellnic as the intercom was picked up somewhere in the building.

'OK, push the door and come up to the first floor,' came the reply.

Mellnic pushed open the huge wooden door and walked into a large hall with an equally large staircase that wound its way up to the various flats.

George Wright had opened his front door and was standing on the landing to take his package from the courier.

'Mr Wright?' asked Mellnic as he walked up the stairs holding out the package in front of him.

'Yes, that's me,' said Wright taking the package from Mellnic.

'Can you sign for it, please,' Mellnic handed a notebook and pen.

As Wright looked down to sign Mellnic removed his gun from his waistband and pointed it at Wright.

'Shall we go in, Mr Wright? We have a lot to talk about,' said Mellnic indicating with the barrel of his gun.

Chapter Fifty-Three

Will and Jay resumed their respective spots across from each other at Will's kitchen table sipping mugs of coffee.

'Wow, that was some twenty four hours,' said Jay how did Dawkin turn up like that?

'Well, I didn't know you would phone Allan but I had a feeling that we were going to need more than just you and me with Michael. So I hedged our bets as I knew Dawkin would arrest us but better that than being dead,' replied Will, 'anyway not sure about twenty four hours more like two months. It seems impossible that it was only eight weeks ago I got the call from Toby asking me to go to Scotland. I wonder how it would all have turned out if I hadn't gone.'

'Some of the events would have undoubtedly turned out the same way, but if you didn't decide that the only way to prove your innocence was to get involved yourself, we may not have caught Bore, certainly not before he had you killed. And who knows we might never have met either,' Jay said with a laugh, 'thank goodness it is all over.'

Will looked pensive.

'What is it Will?'

'I don't know really. There is something at the back of my mind. I have analysed and re-analysed my situation over the last few weeks, tried to make it all make sense. I don't know! It is like one of those flat packed furniture kits, you get to the end and there are a few screws left. You are not sure whether the manufacturer put a few more in, or the kid packing it didn't count properly or you have missed a vital fix and the piece of furniture will collapse. That's how I feel. There is something missing that I can't quite work out. I have a couple of screws that I can't see where they fit.' Will shook his head and made a clicking noise with his mouth. 'Bore said someone in the office had spotted that his businesses were in trouble and he thought that it might have been me originally, but it wasn't, so who?'

'What about Sam or Sara. Both would have had access to Bore's files,' responded Jay.

'Maybe, although generally, for confidentiality purposes, only the partner dealing with a particular client and his or her team can access files.'

'I think you may be a bit paranoid. I am not surprised after all you have been through. Bore has admitted to everything and the police accept that you had nothing to do with any of the murders,' stated Jay.

'Yep, I guess you are right,' replied Will. 'Anyway, it has changed my life entirely. Out with the old and in with the new.' As he smiled and nodded his head in recognition of the situation. 'What about you? What are you going to do Jay?' asked Will.

'Well I have resigned from the Service as I said I would do. Spend more time with my daughter and who knows, really take up photography,' Jay replied holding up the palms of her hands in a questioning way.

'Well, I am going to sell this place,' said Will looking around the kitchen, 'too many bad memories. Thought I might move well away, perhaps to Scotland but that rather depends on one thing.'

'Yes!' said Jay but not in a questioning way but more as a positive response.

Will looked confused.

'Well,' continued Will, 'the one thing is whether you, and of course, your daughter, would consider coming with me?'

Jay said nothing,

'I understand that you might want to take time to consider, speak to your daughter, your parents etcetera,' continued Will hoping to get a response from the silent Jay.

Jay smiled, 'I have just said "Yes".'

'But that was before I asked,' retorted Will.

'Somehow, amongst all this past confusion and betrayal there are some things which are clear and straightforward and that is, how I feel for you,' she said as she stretched her hand across the table and squeezed Will's. 'I think I need to go home and chat to my daughter and my parents about all our futures. Will call you later,' said Jay.

'OK, let me know what everyone thinks. I am flexible about where and when and if your folks want to come I can buy a place big enough for them too,' replied Will.

'OK, will raise the subject but it may take them a while to think this over.'

They kissed goodbye on the front step and Jay walked to her car. Secretly, Jay was on cloud nine, as happy as when her late husband had proposed to her all those years ago. So she didn't notice the fancy car that had suddenly stopped across the road or that it was now following her.

Chapter Fifty-Four

Mellnic closed the door behind him still pointing the gun at George Wright.

'What do you want? I don't keep any money in the flat but I could get you some,' pleaded Wright looking very frightened.

'Don't worry, Mr Wright, I don't intend to kill you, provided you do what I say. Then we will both walk away and forget all this 'appened. However, if you try to call anyone or tell the police, I will kill you,' replied Mellnic.

Mellnic continued.

'I am owed a lot of money, well, in fact, my boss is owed a lot of money but don't think he is in any position to either claim it or use it. So, I am his representative, so to speak.' Mellnic smiled.

'So, what has this to do with me? I don't know who you are talking about or know anything about any money,' stated Wright.

'My boss was owed money by one of your partners, Sam Brewer, but unfortunately he is dead. My only lead is, therefore, to you and the other partners.'

George thought for a few minutes and suspected that this was all to do with Sam impersonating Will.

'I doubt that we will be able to help you,' said George, wanting to know what Mellnic had in mind.

'When we went to collect the money from Brewer's house, one your other partners was there. Slater. I think he knows about the money.'

'I doubt that,' replied Wright starting to think of a plan.

Mellnic pressed the gun into Wright face.

'Don't keep on saying you can't help me or I will just assume you are of no use to me and kill you now.'

'OK, OK. What do you have in mind?' asked Wright.

'I think a trip to Slater's house and perhaps we can persuade him to give us the money.'

George didn't think this was a particularly good plan but decided to play along with it for the moment. He wanted Mellnic out of his house.

'Do you know where he lives?' asked Mellnic.

'Yes, he lives in Wimbledon,' replied Wright.

'Do you have a car?'

'Yes, I have a car' replied George.

'Good, you can drive me there now.'

'How do I know you will not kill me then?' asked George.

'You will have to trust me on this,' replied Mellnic.

George nodded. He picked up his car keys and both men headed down to George's car which was parked around the corner on a residents' parking spot.

Mellnic sat in the passenger seat of George's expensive Bentley convertible.

'Nice car,' said Mellnic.

'I work hard,' replied George.

They drove in silence to Wimbledon and as they reached the road where Will lived, Mellnic said.

'Drive past and show me which house.'

George slowed down as he passed Will's house indicating which one it was. As they passed, the front door opened and Mellnic saw Slater at the front door kissing a very attractive woman.

'Pull in over there,' shouted Mellnic.

Mellnic swivelled in his seat and watched the woman leave the house and get into a small car parked in the road.

'Who is that?' asked Mellnic.

'I don't know, think it might be his new girlfriend,' replied George.

Mellnic formed a plan.

'Follow that car and if you lose it, I will kill you on your lovely leather seat.'

Chapter Fifty-Five

Jay moved around her home tidying up and doing the chores that had been left undone for a few days. She was working out in her mind how to explain to her daughter and her parents that she intended to move to Scotland with a man she hardly knew. She was really happy and looking forward to a new chapter in her life and quietly hummed a tune as she cleaned.

The doorbell rang.

Jay wasn't expecting anyone and suspected it was someone collecting for a charity or trying to sell something. She opened the door wide without the chain and there stood two men, one she recognised but wasn't sure from where and a second man stepped around the first and pointed a gun pointed towards her.

'Step back, please, and keep your hands where I can see them,' Mellnic said.

'Who are you and what do you want?'

'My name is irrelevant but I know you are a friend of, Mr Slater, and you can help me get what was owed to my boss and now to me. Turn around and put your hands against the wall please,' said Mellnic politely but firmly.

Mellnic frisked Jay to make sure there were no weapons concealed about her.

'OK, put your hands behind you.'

Mellnic then tied Jay's hands behind her with plastic cable ties.

'OK, this is what we are going to do. You are going to walk out slowly to the car outside and get into the rear seat and I am going to get in beside you. If you try anything I will kill you. Do you understand?'

'Yes,' replied Jay, 'I understand.' Jay had been trained not to put her life or others in danger and to wait for any opportunity that might occur.

George, Jay and Mellnic walked to George's car and got in.

Chapter Fifty-Six

Will could not get out of his mind "the extra screws" as he had renamed his inability to be entirely satisfied that everything was tied up. To take his mind off the problem, he busied himself writing lists of the things he needed to do to enable him to move. First thing on the list was to place his house on the market for sale. He googled some local estate agents and wrote down their telephone numbers. He would call them in the morning and arrange for them to visit over the next few days to give him an estimate of the sale price and decide which one to use.

Second on the list was to the phone the office and speak to each of the senior associates enquiring where they were in closing the outstanding cases.

Third was to catch up with George Wright. Will looked at his watch, it was late and even George would have left the office by now.

Will sorted our paperwork and paid bills online.

Will was just going to pour himself a glass of wine when the phone rang. He looked at his watch, almost 8.30 p.m.

'Hello,' said Will picking up the receiver.

'It's George, Will, I need to talk to you about Java, could you come around to the office?'

'Can't we talk in the morning when I get in, it is quite late now. I can't believe there is much more to talk about on this subject.'

'It can't really wait Will, I have been with a client all day and have to go back tomorrow morning, big sale very confidential. It won't take long, I need to show you some papers which are here. We could have a late dinner afterwards and talk about the closure of the firm.'

'OK, I suppose so,' said Will looking at his watch again although he knew it was the same time as last time he looked, 'I will get a cab over so I can have a drink with dinner. I will be over as soon as I can.'

'OK, see you soon,' said George cheerily.

Will put the phone down. The extra screws were pricking at his brain again. Will picked up the phone and dialled Jay's home landline. No reply.

He tried her mobile. Still no reply. He thought that strange.

Will made another call and waited.

After a short while the doorbell rang. Will didn't know the man that stood at the door.

'I was asked to bring this over to you. It is simple to fit. Let me show you,' said the stranger.

Will thanked the man who then left.

Will ordered a cab and as soon as it arrived he left for his office.

Chapter Fifty-Seven

Will arrived at the Slater & Craig offices and he could see some of the lights on the third floor were still on. He made his way up to the third floor. He tried the main glass front door but it was locked. He rang the bell and, after a few moments, George arrived in the reception. He looked different somehow, a little dishevelled and sweaty.

'Thanks for coming, Will, let's go into the boardroom, more space,' said George as he strode off into the inner sanctum of the offices.

'Come in, take a seat, Will.'

As Will entered the boardroom, he stopped in horror as in the far corner sitting tied to a chair was Jay with a piece of cloth stuffed into her mouth. He was just about to say something in anger to George when he heard a voice from behind him.

'Welcome, Mr Slater.'

Will turned and faced Mellnic who was pointing a gun at Will's chest.

'Don't do anything stupid, Slater or I will kill you and the girl here,' said Mellnic pointing the barrel of the gun generally in the direction of Jay.

'Sit down.' Mellnic indicated again with his gun to an empty chair at the boardroom table.

Will sat down.

'What the hell is going on here, George and why is Jay here?'

Jay made a gaging noise from the other side of the room.

'George, please take her gag out, she might choke,' pleaded Will.

'You address all your comments to me, Slater,' shouted Mellnic.

'OK, she won't shout, just remove the gag, please,' asked Will.

Mellnic moved across the room and pulled the cloth out of Jay's mouth, who let in a deep breath.

'I recognise you, don't I?' asked Will. 'I know you were at Sam's house, you broke the door down. You are the missing fourth man. How did you get away?'

'That is of no concern to you, Slater,' said Mellnic wagging the gun under Will's nose.

'For God's sake, Mellnic put the gun down on the table and stop waving it about like a cowboy. No one else is armed and neither Slater nor the woman is going to jump at you,' said George.

Mellnic hesitated for a moment.

'I said put it down,' screamed George, 'or I will come over and put it down for you.'

Mellnic looked furious and was going to say something but George was an intimidating figure and Mellnic decided that there was little harm done in abiding by George's order and putting the gun down on the table but in easy reach.

Will and Jay eyes flicked between George and Mellnic during the altercation with some alarm watching to see who was in charge.

'Good, let's all sit down,' said George.

Will was already seated, Mellnic sat towards the end of the table. Close to the door and George on the opposite side of the table from Will.

'I want the money that is owed to my boss,' shouted Mellnic from his seated position banging his palm on the table. 'That's all I came for and I will kill all of you if I don't get it.'

'It's not just about the money, Mellnic. There are other reasons why Slater is here,' said George.

'Not for me there ain't,' said Mellnic raising his bottom off the chair and sliding his hand towards the gun.

George smiled and waved both his hands downwards to indicate that Mellnic should remain seated.

'Of course, there is the money, Mellnic,' said George as he rose putting both hands in his trouser pockets as he sauntered very casually around the table towards Mellnic, 'but we need to cover everything. That is only fair, Mellnic.'

'I don't know what you mean,' he said with a frown but he slumped back in the chair.

George still with his hands in pocket perched his bottom on the edge of the table between Mellnic and Will.

'Now, this is what I think we will do,' said George and with a flash he took his hand out of his pocket picked up the pistol and shot Mellnic in the head.

For a moment, Mellnic had a surprised look on his face and then he was dead.

'Well done, George,' said Will starting to get off his chair.

'Not so fast, Will. Sit down. I meant what I said. This is not all about the money. I have some unfinished business with you,' said George indicating that Will should remain seated.

'What business?' asked Will.

'Whose idea do you think was Java? None of these wankers could have thought this up and managed it by themselves. I was the one with all the connections abroad. I am the one who has been dealing with all these criminal types, while you and the others dealt with the genteel clientele. This was my plan and I am going to finish it.'

'What! I don't understand, what is going on?' But Will now had an inkling that he was about understand where the extra screws were going to fit.

'You are such an arrogant bastard, Will. It was your firm but you treated us all like your slaves so I thought it was time to teach you a lesson. Look at you, your wife runs off with your best mate, your best and oldest client double crosses you and all your partners betray you in some way. What is the connection Will?' said George leaning over Will, his face puce with anger.

'You, you fucker. You. We all hated you!'

Will sat back and shook his head trying to take on-board what George had said.

'You all hated me! That's ridiculous,' cried out Will.

'That's ridiculous,' mimicked George. 'No, it fucking well isn't. It is finished and you and that bitch of yours are finished, too.'

'But I thought Bore was behind it all?' questioned Will.

'He'd had it, overstretched and going bankrupt. A couple of his businesses were failing and he was looking for some quick cash to maintain his lifestyle. You were so arrogant you couldn't even spot that. Just keep billing and collecting the cash with no understanding for anyone else. That's you. I found out and offered him a way out. I told him that he was going to be the middle man with the Eastern Europeans and I didn't exist as far as they were concerned.'

'That was pretty much what he told me, too. But why did he admit it was all him to the police?' asked Will.

'That was our deal. He had nothing. I offered a large sum of money and to keep his villa and his beloved boat for him for when he came out of prison.'

'Why did he trust you?'

'He had little alternative. I told him that if he didn't take the rap, I would see that he was dead before he reached prison. I could do that and he knew it, too. I said I was watching him and provided that he said nothing, I would transfer $500,000 to a bank account and would text the number through to him. When I heard from one of my sources that he had been caught, I texted him the number. He knew that if he talked later, I could just as easily reverse the transfer.'

'So that was your text I heard when we were all kneeling in the hall of my house with the police charging round.'

'Yep, that was me, just reminding him of the deal and it worked well, eh?' replied George smiling to himself.

'But he said all the money was his. He said that that banker Justerini phoned him when I tried to transfer the money.'

'Justerini was also a greedy man and a fool. Yes, he did phone Bore and Bore let me know that you were on the island trying to transfer the funds. But that fool Justerini fucked it up and let the transfer go through. Anyway, he is paying for his inefficiency and stupidity.'

'So you were behind Toby and Sam's death and Foundling's too?' asked Will.

'Well, I didn't pull the triggers but that was the intention, to remove all loose ends. Foundling was a minnow and if you hadn't broken into his office, he would be alive today. So you could say, you killed him. Sam was unfortunate but he was becoming very nervous as was McCloud so I thought the best thing was to finish them off. Of course, I didn't know you were going to be there and bring your gaggle of bodyguards behind you. As it worked out, apart from Mellnic here, everyone who

195

knew anything, died. Just unlucky you escaped too. When I heard you were in a coma I thought that perhaps the gods were on my side after all,' smirked George.

'How did you persuade Sam to be involved in the first place?' asked Will.

'Like Bore, another one whose life was surrounded by huge cash demands. That bitch of a wife bled the poor bastard dry. What with the horses, the holidays and the house. He was desperate for money. I think she had threatened to leave him for some nouveau riche billionaire if he could not support her in the style that she believed she was entitled to. It is a shame she wasn't at home when the bad men came. They might have shot her instead. Sam was a better man than that. I am really sorry that he had to die. I really liked Sam.'

'And Sara?' asked Will.

'Well she was doomed when she married that arsehole Peter. What she saw in him I will never know. You know I think he hit her. I saw some bruises on her back once, she said she had fallen down the stairs. I didn't believe her. She only married him because you wouldn't.'

'What do you mean?'

'She was besotted by you. But you could never see anything past your nose and your ambitions. Then you went and married that betrayer, Claire. That was the last straw for Sara, so she married Peter as she thought that she would not get anyone else at her age having wasted so long hoping you would notice her. We all suspected for years that your wife was being shagged by McCloud and it was only when your children got older that she decided to leave you. Sara always hoped you would find out and leave Claire and she could divorce Peter and marry you. But you were so blind. I sometimes wondered if you had any normal feelings at all.'

Will slumped back in his chair totally deflated by what he was being told.

'Why was Toby involved?' asked Will.

'He was the original financier. We needed some substantial upfront cash to make the first shipment payments. He was always up for a deal. I spun him some yarn and a share in the profits and he was in. He insisted, however, in keeping the password code for the accounts so he could make sure he would get his money and his share back. Initially, he made no enquiries and seemed happy to let "the project", as he called it, grow but then he started to ask more questions about who Java was actually trading with. I had to explain a bit more about the enterprise, not all, but enough to satisfy him. I thought he would be concerned that you were the only director and didn't know what was going on. He actually thought that was rather funny. Anyway some time later he got cold feet and thought that you should be informed and that he wanted out of the whole project. I couldn't allow that so I had to get rid of him. Mellnic's boss was very helpful.'

'And why did you need to kill me?' asked Will.

'You were becoming another lose end. I knew you would not rest after Toby's death and we didn't know what you had found in his house. So Bore and I hatched a plan for you to be killed in Mallorca. Bore said he knew someone who could do it. Waste of time that was, bloody amateur.'

'So you sent the pirates?' asked Will.

'Funnily enough that had nothing to do with us at all. You were just in the wrong place at the wrong time. When I heard I thought it was ironic that you might have been killed accidently. We tried again in Scotland, but that bitch,' said George indicating in the direction of Jay, 'got in our way. I even got that idiot Crombie to push you under a train after we had met at the Grenadier but he couldn't even do that properly,' George rocked back on his feet and laughed out loud. 'Imagine having been a soldier most of your life and surviving tours in Iraq and Afghanistan and then being shot by your own wife.' George laughed again loudly. 'I am surrounded by fools.'

'What about all the money in Java? You can't get that. You don't know where it is? Only I do,' stated Will.

'Ah, ha, now, we are back to your real love, the money. I have got plenty more stashed away. That is the benefit of working for shady people they are happy with unorthodox methods of payment. Besides, who is to say that I won't work out where you have put the rest of the cash when you are dead,' replied George.

'And how are you going to get away?'

'That is probably the simplest part of the plan to date. I kill you both. I leave in the car waiting downstairs, catch an

197

evening flight to somewhere that I am not telling you. By the time they find you in the morning, I will be half-way across the world with a different name and a different lifestyle. All part of a corporate financier's planning expertise.'

'OK, seems as if that is it for me but Jay is not part of your hate for me. Can't you at least let her go? Leave her tied up until the morning and your plan would still work but with one less body on your conscious.'

George tilted his head to one side as if in thought.

'I don't think so, as I suspect this creature would hunt me down to the corners of the earth for revenge. I'm afraid she must go too,' replied George.

'OK, George, guess that was your last chance to show some humility. There is something I need to show you,' Will's hands moved down to his jacket.

'Not so fast, just keep your hands where I can see them.'

'OK, just the left hand,' and Will held open his jacket to reveal a little black clip attached to his shirt.

'What's that?' exclaimed George.

'I believe it is called a microphone, George. SO 15 have heard every word you have said. I am afraid it is all over for you, old boy.' Will emphasizing the "old boy" in a cynical voice.

They all heard the outer office door being opened with a bang.

'If I go, so do you, you arrogant bastard,' shouted George.

As George raised his gun, he failed to see the little red spot reflected on his shirt hovering over his heart. George never got to squeeze the trigger. In fact, he never breathed again as the window glass shattered and a small object from the office over the road entered George's chest at the exact place indicated by the red spot. As George dropped to the floor, Harry Allan and colleagues rushed into the boardroom with guns raised.

'It's OK, he's dead,' said Will and jumped up to go over to Jay.

'Scissors, I need scissors or something to cut these ties,' shouted Will.

A pair was placed into Will's hands and he released Jay from her bondage. She flew into his arms and cried.

'It's all over now, really over. They are all dead or in custody,' said Will as he comforted Jay's shaking body.

'Your mates Don Quixote and Pancha Sanchez will be here soon,' said Allan. 'Why don't you two push off home? I will take the flak for letting you go. Think you both deserve it.'

'OK, we will. We can get a cab in the street.' Will took Jay's arm who was still visibly upset by the ordeal and helped her out of the offices.

Chapter Fifty-Eight

Will and Jay, once again, sat opposite each other across the kitchen table.

'Do you really think it is all over now?' asked Jay. 'I keep thinking it is and then there is another episode. It is just like an awful nightmare, where you keep walking into rooms that you know are frightening but you just can't stop until it is too late or you wake yourself up.'

'I think it must be. There is no one left now,' replied Will with a little laugh.

'There a few things I don't understand. Why were you wearing a wire and how did Allan know where we were?'

'You know when I gave you an analogy about the missing screws.'

'Yes, I remember,' replied Jay.

'Well, it was still worrying me and then George phoned me and asked me to meet him with a poor excuse as to why it couldn't wait and suddenly the penny dropped, or to continue with my analogy, I could see where the extra screws had to go. I told you that I had been analysing and re-analysing everything and I started making a list of everything that had happened including the smallest detail. Reliving every day, even every hour, from the moment that I woke up on that fateful Saturday morning.

'The first thing that I thought strange was when I went to the office to have a meeting with Michael Bore. I went out to make some coffee and when I came back, he was standing in my office but I had the feeling that he had been doing something. I don't know what. He said something strange to me, too. He said and I remember it quite clearly, '*Sometimes, Will, everything is not what it seems and you should take advice from your friends.*' I thought nothing of it, Michael was a strange man and I could never fully make him out. When he left, I walked around the office and that was when I saw an empty folder half-stuck out of George's desk. The folder had the name Java PLC on it. Once again, I thought nothing of it, although George was meticulous and I thought it strange that he would leave his desk in that manner. Events overtook me and I had forgotten about that episode until I starting writing it all down.'

'So what do you think it meant?' asked Jay.

'Well, I think Michael was warning me about George, but didn't dare to do it openly. Michael certainly has business savvy and he would always "sail close to the wind" if it was to his advantage but he wasn't a criminal. It always seemed strange that he was the big boss behind this whole operation.'

'George said that Bore's business empire was failing. Why didn't he come to you to discuss it? How did George find out about it?' asked Jay.

'Yes, that has been puzzling me, too. I am sure I could have come up with a plan to help ease the problem if he had asked. Michael was a very proud man and I had known him for years and I had said that I admired his business acumen. I wonder if he just didn't want to admit to me that he had made some mistakes. Then when I was in Bore's villa, there was an entry in the visitors' book from George and I recalled him having done some work for him. The visit to the villa must have been a thank you. So, perhaps, Michael felt more comfortable approaching George with his financial difficulties rather than me!'

'There must have been something else, too,' probed Jay.

'Yes, there was, when I broke into Foundling's office, I was flicking through the correspondence files in his filing cabinet looking for my name, as there weren't that many, they all sort of flopped forward in the cabinet as I worked my way from the back of the row, my eyes caught sight of a file with the name "G. Wright". Not an unusual name but I remember George had quite a humble background and grew up in South London and was always very loyal to the people that he dealt with in his early days and I put two and two together. So when I got the call from George this evening, and after not being able to contact you, which I thought strange, I was worried and I phoned Allan. He was also concerned and when I explained it all, he said that he agreed with my analysis. He said he thought that Bore had confessed too easily to everything. Allan thought there was every likelihood that Wright might try and kill me again. He asked whether I would be happy to carry a microphone so that they could record what was said. I agreed as I didn't think for a minute George would expect such a thing. He said he would provide backup if things got nasty. I didn't know what would happen and although I was worried about you, I didn't think that George had kidnapped you, so I was horrified when I walked into the boardroom to see you tied up. I thought all I could do was play along with George, who I thought I could probably handle, but Mellnic added a different dimension to the scenario. When George shot him I really thought that we were in the clear and that George had been forced into kidnapping you by Mellnic. But then I realised that Mellnic and his boss must have been employed by George all along. He was really a tough nut. He came from a tough background and I suppose it never leaves you.'

'Do you think George and Mellnic were in it together all along?' asked Jay.

'No, I don't think so. Mellnic may have seen George, through his dealings with Mellnic's boss, in the early days of this deal, but I think they both saw an opportunity to use each other for their own ends. Mellnic thought he was the tough guy but he didn't know who he was dealing with,' replied Will.

'What are you going to do with the money?' asked Jay.

'To be honest, I am not sure. Technically the money is mine. It is in my name, transferred from a company that I owned. The company has paid all its tax so those authorities will not be interested. I will seek some legal advice but I have a mind to make some donations to charities, set up an anonymous trust fund for Sara and Sam's children and then, I suppose, keep the rest. It is not that I shouldn't be owed something for all this. It has been quite horrendous. Well, I will wait to see if anyone enquires as to its existence and if they do, will consider the validity of their claim. As I see it, we have both earned it over the last few weeks. I call it a down payment on our future together,' replied Will.

'Some down payment. George was correct, you are very focused on money. Let's hope it won't come back to haunt us in the future,' replied Jay as she stretched her hand across the table and squeezed Will's and repeated, 'Yes let's hope it won't come back and haunt us.'

Chapter Fifty-Nine

Dawkin was sitting at his desk, with his arms crossed, staring into space when Edgar knocked on the open door and entered.

'You OK, Gov?' enquired the Sergeant.

'Ummm, not sure,' replied Dawkin, 'it all fits together too well.'

'What does?' asked Edgar.

'The Slater business.'

'Well, surely that is the idea, isn't it? We find a suspect and then he admits to the crime and we bang him up,' replied Edgar, 'then we get even luckier as the bloke who set up the whole shebang gets gunned down by SO 15. We get the credit and SO 15 walks into the sunset.'

'Yea, but apart from Bore in jail, everyone else is dead, apart from Slater, that is. Very convenient, if you ask me. Cases don't usually tie up like that, in my experience.'

'But you were complaining that there were too many lose ends, and now, we don't have any, you are complaining again.'

'Yea, I was,' said Dawkin dreamily, continuing to stare into space, 'but you know that Slater is a very clever man and I think I may have underestimated him.'

'That's unlike you, Gov, but I do think you are getting paranoid about this case, perhaps it is your age,' replied Edgar.

'Maybe, maybe, and anyway who are you calling old,' responded Dawkin.

Chapter Sixty

Will went back to his list of things to do for his move. Jay had spoken to her daughter and subject to meeting Will, was happy to move to Scotland to be with her mother, although she had built up a strong relationship with her grandparents and would visit them each school holiday. Jay's parents thanked him for the offer for them to move, too, but decided that at their time of life a move would be too unsettling and they were looking forward to time to themselves.

Will would need to spend another couple of months closing down the firm and attending Michaela Bore's trial as a witness but during that time, Jay and he would visit Scotland and look for a suitable house for the three of them to live.

With more money than Will would need, the future looked rosy.

Chapter Sixty-One

A few days later, Dawkin was sitting at his desk dealing with a new case, when the phone rang.

'Hello, Dawkin,' he said.

There was a slight pause, 'Ah, Mr Dawkin, my name is Chris Melody, I am with the Financial Services Commission in the British Virgin Islands.'

'Oh, how can I help you, Mr Melody.'

'We have been investigating a man called Justerini, following a tip-off, as to his banking activities on these islands. He was involved in a case that I believe you were dealing with involving a London Solicitor called Will Slater.'

'Yes, that is correct,' said Dawkin sitting up in his chair suddenly more interested in the call.

'We found a sheet of paper in Justerini's desk, which was headed Java PLC and had just two telephone numbers on it. The first number belonged to a Michael Bore, whom we understand has been arrested under terrorism charges in the UK. The second number is not traceable. Pay as you go, I imagine,' stated Melody.

'Ummm,' said Dawkin in a questioning way, 'and...?'

'As far as I can tell from the reports that I have read, everyone involved in the case is either in detention or dead,' replied Melody.

'That is correct, with one exception I suppose,' said Dawkin, thinking about Slater.

'Well I have just phoned the number and it was picked up but with no answer.'

'I knew it, I knew it,' shouted Dawkin, 'he has made fools of us all.'

The End

If you want to read the sequel to this book, it will be out next year and is called **Revenge**.